Condor

A Novel

Perry — thanks for your
support. Hope you enjoy!

Jimbo 4/22

James Bell

Also by James Bell

The Screen Door: A Story of Love, Letters
and Travel

The Twenty-Year Chafe

Christchurch

Crisis in the Congo

American Dreamer

Spook

Santiago, Chile

September 11, 1973

"It's Salvador," she whispered, opening her eyes and checking the clock. It was 6:22 in the morning.

Isabel Letelier handed the telephone to her husband. The new minister of defense sat up in bed. He'd managed only three hours of sleep, worried about intelligence reports of an imminent coup.

"The navy has revolted," announced President Allende to her husband, Orlando Letelier. "Six truckloads of navy troops are on their way to Santiago from Valparaiso. The Carabineros are the only units that respond. The other commanders in chief don't answer the phone. Pinochet doesn't answer. Find out what you can." Allende paused, exhaling audibly over the phone. "Go Orlando, and take control of the Defense Ministry if you can get there."

At 7:30 Letelier arrived, unarmed, at his ministry. The streets were empty, except for military vehicles, his military's vehicles. A late winter mist hung over the dimly-lit edifice off the Alameda Bernardo O'Higgins. Troops had surrounded the building as he got out of his limousine and strode toward the entrance. A guard at the front door halted his progress as another voice barked, "Let the Minister in." As Letelier entered, he felt the sharp end of a rifle butt poke his ribs.

Orlando Letelier stared at twelve jumpy young men in army uniforms pointing machine guns at him. "Take him downstairs," ordered the one who looked to be in charge. Letelier was hustled down a flight of stairs to the basement, where he was searched and thrown against a wall in a small meeting room. "I demand to see the senior officer."

Another uniformed man entered the room and approached Letelier, sticking his beefy face three inches from the Defense Minister. "Look, sir, if you insist on this, we'll proceed immediately to execute you."

That afternoon, guards took Letelier to an infantry regiment in southern Santiago and locked him in a tiny lightless room. Through cracks in the slats of the drawn wooden shutters, he watched hooded men being brought in and taken out through the evening. At least twenty of them were dragged from the barracks into the parade yard pleading for their lives. All night long, he could hear angry threats and voices of fear, the barking orders and muted replies fading into cold silence. The muzzled sound of a rifle occasionally pierced the night, causing Letelier to worry about the long day ahead. Just before five in the morning, he heard a voice outside his room. "Now it's the Minister's turn." A half-hour later, the door opened.

"Come on," the guard motioned. Letelier walked along the corridor, then down another flight of steps, accompanied by six soldiers. One of them took the towel he was carrying, fashioned it into a blindfold and put it over Letelier's eyes. He recoiled and glared at the young man. The boy showed neither fear nor respect for the Minister of Defense. *What has this world come to?* They stopped at the end of the hallway, as two guards saluted the superior officer. There was a brief discussion between the officer and the guards, before the senior officer announced, "Take the prisoner up again."

The young guard whispered to Letelier, "You've lucked out asshole. They're not going to off you, you bastard."

Dawson's Island, Chile

The next day Orlando Letelier and three dozen other senior Allende officials were flown eight hours south on a DC-6 plane to Puente Arenas, then transported five hours on a military ship to Dawson's Island, a bleak outpost across the Strait of Magellan at the tip of the continent. He had not shaved or changed clothes in five days, nor had he smoked a cigarette. That was no easy task for a man who regularly inhaled four packs per day.

The concentration camp where Letelier and his fellow political prisoners were taken was fenced off by a double row of barbed wire and patrolled by guards armed with antiaircraft guns from watchtowers. He lived in a 8-by-15-foot room with seven other men, sleeping in three-tier bunks with scratchy sheets. They called it 'El Sheraton.'

Guards woke the prisoners at 6 a.m. to begin twelve-hour days building latrines, reinforcing barbed wire, and cutting firewood. Letelier and other senior Allende officials were routinely yanked out of their beds in the middle of the night and forced to stand in the rain or snow. Frequently they were thrown into the mud and left to shiver in freezing temperatures all night long. Letelier remained stoic, even humorous, keeping his fellow prisoners' spirits up by teaching English, singing and playing guitar. Still, he lost fifty pounds in the first three months, with his weight on his rangy 6"3" frame dropping to 125 pounds. The worst of the suffering was psychological. Guards routinely lined up and blindfolded the men at all hours of the day and night, taunting them about being shot. The new Pinochet regime enjoyed degrading the senior officials of the Allende government.

By mid-1974, various international organizations began putting direct pressure on the Pinochet government. The U.N. Human Rights Commission called the treatment of the Dawson's prisoners 'barbaric sadism' and the International Red Cross found Orlando Letelier 'to be in very bad condition.' He was finally transferred to a hospital in Puente Arenas to treat his malnutrition, then flown to Ritique, a coastal resort north of Santiago that had been repurposed into an upscale concentration camp for senior Allende officials. The prisoners remained restricted in their activities, but were allowed weekly visitors and recreation time, during which they could talk with family and friends or play chess. One family friend who visited Letelier at Ritique was Diego Arria, the governor of Caracas, Venezuela. He had stopped by prior to a meeting the next

through the carved wooden front door, festooned with bright lights and neon signs for Dos Equis beer. The air conditioning was rattling. The room was dark and smelled of Clorox. A small man behind the bar shoveling ice from the machine into a bucket waved him toward a booth near the back of the restaurant, where two dark-haired men sat. A thick woman shuffled over, her front gold tooth agleam, and placed three laminated menus on the table. After the obligatory small talk about families and mutual friends, Virgilio Paz asked, "What's up?"

"Orders," Townley answered. "This is something heavy."

"No problem. But you aren't the most popular man around here with the Cuban community, you know? This may not be the right time," said Paz. Virgilio Paz was in his late-twenties, wiry and handsome, with a neat beard. He moved to New Jersey in the late fifties from Cuba and was the youngest member of the Cuban Nationalist Movement. He dressed neatly and Townley noticed his buffed, brown woven leather shoes.

"I know," Townley replied. "Hear me out."

"Is it in Europe?" asked Guillermo Novo. The urbane older man had emigrated from Cuba in the mid-fifties with his younger brother, Ignacio. The Novo brothers were active opponents of the Castro regime, and were arrested for firing a bazooka at the United Nations Building in the early 1960s when Che Guevara was speaking to the General Assembly. Novo had shiny, groomed black hair and grey sideburns on his round face, along with a tic that caused his right cheek to quiver. His eyes and head moved often as he talked, giving him a slightly crazed manner.

"No," said Townley. "It's in Washington."

Paz barely raised an eyebrow. "Who?"

"One of Allende's cabinet ministers," said Townley. "A guy named Letelier. He's a Marxist and is forming a government in exile. He must be eliminated."

Guillermo Novo jumped in, aggravated at the treatment of their colleague in Venezuela. "Here's the deal," he answered, after Townley laid out the terms of the hit. Townley would reimburse them up to $1500 for the materials needed and any travel expenses incurred up to $750, although the hit was being done gratis. "We'll do it, but want to know what you'll do. This is a partnership, after all."

"What do you propose?"

"You have to participate and be there. You have to go down to Washington yourself. We want a signal that this will be a more equal partnership."

"That is contrary to my orders," answered Townley.

"I thought your orders were to get the job done."

"They are," said Townley. "But I'm not supposed to go to Washington."

"That's what we don't like," said Novo. "So, you better try to get your orders changed. Because if you leave now, it's not going down. It's that simple. Our movement wants the hand of Chile very close to the act. You put the bomb on. We will set it off. That seems like a fair partnership to us."

On September 16th, Virgilio Paz and the Novo brothers drove from New Jersey to D.C., where they checked into a Holiday Inn in northwest Washington. They spent the next two days surveilling Letelier, waiting at the Roy Rogers on River Road a few blocks from his home in Bethesda, then following his blue Chevelle into the District. Novo bought wire cutters, needle-nose pliers, a soldering iron, slide switches, and a blasting cap at a Radio Shack in Jersey City. Paz obtained the detonating cord and pager, a small piece of C-4 putty, and TNT from CNM associates in the New York area. Michael Townley drove separately and checked into the nearby Regency Congress hotel as 'Kenneth Enyart,' a LAN-Chile pilot. They agreed to meet at Townley's hotel to assemble the bomb on Sunday, place it that night underneath Letelier's car, and detonate it Monday morning while he drove to work. Townley's job was to affix the bomb under the driver's seat and mold the plastique to blow the full explosive force directly upright.

Shortly after midnight, Townley and the Cubans drove to Bethesda and found Letelier's Chevelle parked in the driveway, nose in. The job consisted mostly of fitting the C-4 putty into a baking pan between chunks of TNT. Townley hid the baking pan under his shirt and lay down underneath the driver's side of the vehicle. He began to tape the pan to the A-frame, when he heard a car approach with its radio on. He froze, noticing the car was a police cruiser. The cruiser turned the corner and drove away. Townley exhaled. He continued taping the pan to the crossbeam and made sure the slide switch on the bomb was on, then secured the pan with the remainder of his roll of duct tape. The explosives would concentrate their blast directly upward toward Letelier's legs.

"It's not going anywhere, except straight up," he reassured the Cubans as they drove back to their hotels. "Remember to detonate the device when Letelier is alone. You should do it in a park where no bystanders would be injured or killed."

All Virgilio Paz had to do was place his finger on the two buttons of the detonator and, at the right time, plug it into the cigarette lighter.

Two

Washington, D.C. and Alexandria, VA.

September 21, 1976

William McKenzie Thomas, Jr. – Willie, or Willie Mac to his close friends – was not much of a student. As a child, Willie was well-liked and curious; teachers remarked on his potential. "He's bright, but easily distracted." He'd heard that since kindergarten. Follow through had always been his shortcoming. Today, Willie would be tagged with ADHD and provided with a cornucopia of pills.

After five years, Willie had earned his degree in English from GW, although he imagined doing little with it. His parents framed the diploma and now it sat in a neat pile on his dresser, along with other forgotten citations for childhood accomplishments. The last few years had been particularly forgettable. The United States was still in a stupor two years after Nixon resigned. President Ford kept talking about 'win-ning' – an awkward acronym for *whipping inflation now.* Malaise, either Willie's or the country's, was the real problem. Maybe the upcoming election could put things on a better course?

Some of his friends urged him to 'go west' – or go waste, as James Mitchener suggested. *Work as a lift operator at Snowmass.* An easy, mindless job to fit his restless mood. A high school friend was heading out next month. The truth was that William Thomas didn't know where to go, nor had any clue about what he wanted to do. Unemployment stood at 8% and getting through college had been the only goal so far in his life. Willie received an English degree like everyone else who didn't get a history degree. He enjoyed reading and could be a fountain of useless, sometimes entertaining information, but none of it put him on a path to a career or adulthood. He didn't even know what to call himself. Willie or Willy Mac had worked so far, but neither were adult names. Will or Mac were more professional, although Mac sounded like someone working on a loading dock. Getting his name straight was just another issue to figure out. If Willie had known that growing up and getting a real job required so much effort and planning, he'd have headed west long before now.

Willie wished he possessed his older sister's ambition and focus. Beryl Thomas was one of those people who always got things done without muss or fuss. She graduated with the first class of women at UVa in 1973 and was now working for an investment bank in New York. Willie admired his big sister, but he grew tired of being compared to her. She did everything right without effort. Beryl had a calm answer for every situation and was an early proponent of her brother's western walkabout plans. "Life is long, nothing matters before you are twenty-five. The rat race will be waiting and the line's shorter. Travel of a certain length puts you at the front of it."

Willie looked forward to the first day of Autumn. He liked cooler weather and was worn out by the long hot summer that crept along breathlessly. D.C. was a sweat pit in summer and the heat never completely lifted until the Halloween costumes came out. His father, Big Bill, set him up with a good family friend who worked in commercial real estate. "I don't care if you work in real estate or not. Get some interviewing practice," he repeated many times over the summer. "You have to start somewhere. Barnes, Morris & Pardoe is the leading commercial real estate firm in D.C. and you'll learn how to sell something. C'mon son, focus."

Willie's parents were full of suggestions. Selling something was the mantra. "Be prepared if someone challenges you to sell them a ballpoint pen. Have your spiel down," his father lectured. Willie understood that the exercise was about thinking on his feet, but he didn't give a shit about pens or commercial real estate. At least he learned to type, although he wisely didn't sell that as a marketable skill to his father. "David wants to meet you for a coffee at the Ritz Carlton. It's on Massachusetts Avenue at 21st Street, between DuPont and Sheridan Circle. Give yourself enough time to find street parking. Traffic can be a mess." Big Bill remembered his friend David telling him, "As D.C. grows from a sleepy Southern town into a world capital, commercial real estate is directly in the path of progress. A lot of folks are going to be making a lot of money." Big Bill loved this kind of enthusiasm. As a child of the Depression and veteran of World War II, he grabbed everything that was put down in front of him and sorted it out later.

Willie admired his father, but didn't share his straightforward view of 'a career.' He understood his father's opinion on the value of a profession, particularly now that he had a college degree. Willie had listened to countless lectures on self-reliance and responsibility, but his head was still muddled. In low moments, Willie wondered if his dad was right. Maybe he was spoiled and lazy? He heard his father use those terms many times growing up. There was little tolerance for 'aimless exploration' that this generation reportedly indulged in. But Willie just couldn't get his head around making a career decision. He needed to get out of town. Beryl agreed and she helped work their parents over. Her imprimatur really counted, particularly with their dad. She too quoted Michener about the value of a real life experience before a career, 'go waste young man' was a counter message of the times. Beryl could even get away with comparing her father getting a Purple Heart in World War II to her brother's walkabout plans.

Virgilio Paz and Guillermo Novo had spent the last few days learning Orlando Letelier's morning route from Ogden Court in Bethesda into the District. Letelier drove faster than most of the traffic and the men lost him for a few moments on the first trip in. But he took the same route both days, leaving his house at 8:40 one morning, 8:55 the next. Today they were anxious. Last night, they had cross words with the tall DINA guy about his involvement. Townley originally wanted them to take on the full operation, but that wasn't right or fair. In these kinds of operations, everyone's fingers need to be a little dirty. Paz also worried that the bomb might fall off the cheap cross beam suspension of the Chevy on the drive into town. Townley assured them the tape was strong. It wasn't going anywhere, except straight up into the driver. The plan was set and Townley was already at JFK getting ready to board his flight to Miami. Paz and Novo would wait for Letelier at Roy Rogers and follow him as far as the line at the minipark on 46th Street. At that point, Virgilio Paz would press the remote-control detonation button. Letelier should be alone, Townley had instructed.

"There he is," Novo cried out, pointing as Letelier drove by, window down, laughing and talking a mile a minute. "Looks like someone else is in the car. Shit!" Through the drizzle, it appeared there were three people in the car. "The only one supposed to be in the vehicle is Letelier," Novo protested. "Goddammit." There was an eerie silence as Novo drove ahead, three cars behind the Chevelle. He began to tap his thumbs on the steering wheel, restless and agitated.

"We go ahead," Paz said firmly, sitting in the passenger seat, fingers fiddling with the flat metal device in his lap. "This mission goes ahead. The rest is on DINA to clean up. Let's get this over with."

Orlando Letelier was running late, as usual. He intended to leave his house in Bethesda by eight-thirty to pick up two colleagues on the way into town. It was almost nine and Monday morning traffic headed into the District was heavy. Two years in Washington hadn't changed his habitual tardiness, although he was far better here than at home. Letelier rolled down the window in his 1975 blue Chevelle Malibu Classic to blow out the last puffs of cigarette smoke. He needed to get the smell out of the car, or the entire conversation into the District will be over quitting smoking. He was heading south on Wisconsin Avenue to pick up Ronni Moffitt, a twenty-five year old fund raiser for the IPS, and her husband of three months, Michael, an economist for the Institute. Letelier was fond of the couple; in particular Ronni who brought light and laughter into the quiet think tank on Sheridan Circle. She liked to tease her boss, who was well-known for his flirtations with women and passion for what he did. It was a grey and muggy with drizzle, as Ronni opened the front passenger window. "I smell that you've been smoking in this car again this morning," she teased, buckling herself into the front passenger seat. "I thought you were going to quit? Don't you listen to the ads on TV?"

"Next week," he promised, nodding his head at the familiar refrain. "I'm waiting for that nicotine gum to come out. I hear it works." He lowered the window again and shrugged. "What can I say? I'm working on it." He rolled the window all of the way down and rechecked the air conditioning.

Ronni had been on him for nearly a year to quit, but Orlando Letelier rarely made it a whole day without a cigarette. Dawson's Island was the last place he was forced to do that. He felt comfortable in Washington. America could be a messy, violent place, but there was an order to the system and democracy generally worked. The press was

call Mr. DeCamp. But first, he needed to get out of this mess.

Willie inched his way northwest along Massachusetts Avenue to DuPont Circle, but at that point traffic cops had sealed off Mass Avenue and directed everyone south on 19ᵗʰ Street. *Early reports from the scene indicate a car bomb exploded on Embassy Row and there are casualties. Stay tuned to WTOP.* "A car bomb?" Willie asked himself, shaking his head. "On Embassy Row?" Groups of police cars and emergency vehicles kept rolling toward the accident. Sirens and harsh amplified voices of policemen directing cars to pull over to let emergency vehicles go by was the soundtrack that Monday morning.

After nearly an hour, he crossed the Memorial Bridge back into Virginia, exiting south at the GW Parkway. Stunned, not sure what to make of the news, Willie drove home to Old Town. He needed to call Mr. DeCamp. It was steamy after the rain and the late summer smell of the Tidal Basin forced him to roll the window back up. Willie continued searching the radio dial for more news on what had happened. *'A bomb went off this morning at Sheridan Circle. Police and FBI are investigating. A Chilean foreign national and an American were killed in the blast. More details to come.'*

Willie didn't know what to make of what he'd heard. He spoke basic high school Spanish and had made a few Latin American friends at GW, two Peruvians and a Colombian, but knew nothing about Chile. He remembered hearing about a military coup a few years ago that killed the socialist president. Besides that, he heard Chile was a beautiful country with a lot of copper and a great ski resort called Portillo. Maybe he could go there and be a lift operator?

Willie pulled into the driveway on South Fairfax Street. The sticky drizzle only made him more irritable. His new Joseph Bank suit and pressed button-down shirt had lost shape and clung to him like cellophane. He couldn't wait to take it off. Willie felt like he was trying out for a school play, all dressed in an unfamiliar outfit. His once promising athletic build had softened since an unremarkable high school athletic career ended. He longed for shorts and a tee shirt.

No one was home except for Alma, the housekeeper. She and Willie had a friendly, teasing relationship and he occasionally practiced rudimentary Spanish with her. They rarely discussed politics, although she might know something about Chile. Weren't all those countries next to each other?

"¿Escuchaste?" Willie screamed over the vacuum cleaner. "Did you hear?" he tried again.

Alma looked up at Willie, shaking her head. She cut off the vacuum cleaner and stared towards him. "No William, I haven't heard anything. In case you didn't notice, I'm vacuuming the floor. The machine is very loud." She looked down, then up toward Willie. "You're dressed up. Job interview?"

"Well, yes, but a bomb went off where my interview was. So, I need to reschedule it."

"A bomb? What kind of bomb?"

"I don't know. I think a car bomb. They said on the radio that a Chilean guy and a woman were killed. On Embassy Row. Must be diplomat types."

Alma's face went still, her usual wiseass routine with Willie suddenly halted. "Turn on the TV," she said pointing to the console in the den.

Local coverage of the explosion on Embassy Row identified the casualties of the explosion as Orlando Letelier, 44, a Chilean national working for an international think tank, who had been the ambassador to the U.S. and Defense Secretary under Salvador Allende, and Ronni Moffit, 25, an American fundraiser for the organization. Her husband, Michael survived with minimal injuries. The pictures of the mayhem, firehoses and remains of a blue Chevelle littered the Circle. Gnarled car parts were scattered everywhere and pieces of leatherette, matted against steaming, oily metal scraps, were strewn across the pavement. Cheap molded foam bits, weighted by transmission fluid, sat on the street like wet confetti after a parade. What was left of the carburetor ended in a trail of blood on the sidewalk. There were tiny pieces of something stuck in the trees above the blast. The entire area was cordoned off with yellow tape.

"That's the work of Pinochet," Alma explained over the television coverage. "The Chilean was a political figure, an Allende guy. But he was an economist, and a diplomat." She looked over at Willie matter-of-factly. "These military guys are crazy. He's done it in Argentina and Uruguay, too." She shook her head in disgust at the television.

Willie gazed at Alma. She was a small handsome woman who cleaned their house for the past four years. She dressed modestly in a white uniform, but she had the bearing of an educated worldly woman who had known privilege as a child. Alma had warm brown eyes and her hair was cut stylishly short around her round pale face. They had a friendly teasing relationship, although Willie sensed her disappointment in him and his lack of ambition and curiosity. Alma's young daughters were already more knowledgeable about the world than Willie. She had gotten him a graduation card, wishing him the best of luck in pursuing his dreams. That he had no clue about what those dreams were made him unsettled. Did everyone have their life figured out at age twenty-three?

"South America is a mess," she continued. "At least the southern part where I'm from is. Chile, Uruguay, Argentina. The military controls everything now. My family left when the president declared a state of emergency in 1968. We were lucky to get out. Ordinary people just disappearing. People your age."

"What do you mean *disappearing?*"

"The ones who are politically active, or express an opinion contrary to the leaders, are considered enemies. The man who was killed was tortured in a prison camp for over a year. He was Chile's ambassador to the United States. An internationally respected economist. He wasn't some Che Guevara character."

She paused. "Most everyone knows someone who has been taken by the military. We call them the *desaparecidos*, the missing, the disappeared. Young people are being rounded up and shot … or tortured … sometimes dropped out of helicopters." She threw her hands up in a helpless gesture.

"Do you know someone?" Willie asked. This was all news to him. *Dropping young people out of helicopters?* He vaguely remembered news stories about leftist revolutionaries trying to take over Chile a few years earlier.

Alma frowned. "Unfortunately, I do. My niece, Marcela. She and her husband disappeared last month. They live in Buenos Aires. They were walking home from work, when two men grabbed and shoved them into a car. They haven't been seen since. That's all we know."

Willie Thomas never endured hardship, and certainly hadn't learned many lessons in his uneventful life. He was raised in a comfortable upper middle class home in Old Town Alexandria and underachieved his way through GW. He did what was expected, but little more, viewing his college years as a time to enjoy himself and learn to live eight miles away from home. He had spent his entire life in the ample shadow of Beryl, who did everything right. 'Success' was pounded into Willie's head, even though its definition – the attainment of wealth, favor or fame – was never really explained, nor had much appeal for Willie. It felt good to ask genuine questions he was embarrassed to ask his parents. It was too late for that now.

This crash course in South American current affairs was new. Like most U.S. college graduates, William Thomas was clueless about his continental neighbors. He heard that it was wild with big rivers and mountains and endless plains full of cattle. He knew about the Incas and the conquistadors; that Butch Cassidy went to Bolivia and died in a shootout; that Brazilians spoke Portuguese and were good at soccer; and that most countries had right-wing military dictatorships. On TV, these jowly old men in sunglasses wore lots of medals and epaulets on their pressed uniforms. But South America was a long way from here and if America helped avert a civil war with a lot of deaths, like what just happened in Viet Nam, so be it.

Willie went upstairs to his room to take off his suit. The conversation with Alma irritated him. Here he was a recent college graduate who couldn't even hold a basic conversation about South America with his housekeeper. Willie had taken the coffee table atlas up to his room to look at the geography and began to leaf through his old collection of World Book encyclopedias. *Where's Uruguay? No, that's Paraguay. There it is. Buenos Aires is right across the bay? Or is that a river?* He studied the map. This was the first time he'd ever looked at South America. It was a big lopsided waffle ice cream cone. Chile slivered for 2500 miles down the west coast to the tip at Cape Horn. Argentina, to the east, was four times larger and had very few people outside a half-dozen cities. The country was spacious and the climate was temperate. Santiago and Buenos Aires appeared stylish and European with their wide boulevards, snappily-dressed people, and classical architecture. The far south had been settled and farmed by Europeans – the Welsh and Irish, Germans, Italians, some

Croatians, and the English. The pictures of the landscapes, with their emptiness, glaciers and sheep surprised him. It was completely different from the ugly chaotic cities to the north, like Sao Paulo and Caracas that he occasionally saw smoldering on the news. He picked up the phone in the hallway.

"Mr. DeCamp? Hi, Will Thomas. I'm sorry about today …."

"No need to say anything," he jumped in quickly. "We all heard the explosion. What a mess! I tried calling your dad to postpone our talk."

"I got as far as DuPont Circle, but the police made me turn around. Can we reschedule at some point?"

"Of course. I heard it was a Chilean diplomat and two others. I think they were Americans who worked for him."

"That's what I heard, too. Scary times we live in. How about early next week when things calm down?"

"No problem."

Willie hung up the phone and went back into his bedroom. He began to thumb through the atlas, noticing how little of the world he'd seen. He wasn't sure what he was going to ask Mr. DeCamp anyway. He had no interest in working in commercial real estate. He told his parents that, but he was still living under their roof, and rules. All he wanted was to go somewhere else to figure things out.

There had to be better places than his bedroom in his parents' home.

Willie heard the droning sound of the vacuum cleaner downstairs. Even his housekeeper had seen and done more interesting things than him ... and with all his advantages. Her family moved lock, stock and barrel 5,000 miles to Washington with three children and little else nearly a decade ago. They were smart, educated people from a small town an hour north of Montevideo, who kept their heads down and avoided the ongoing political drama. "If you want to speak out about your country, you can't," Alma had said several times without explanation over the years. "But in America, you can. You can do anything." Willie wasn't sure. The Chilean guy who got blown up was a political opponent of the current government and he was killed nine miles from here.

Three

Washington, D.C. and Buenos Aires, Argentina

Late September-December, 1976

Carter Cornick and Eugene Propper were an odd pair from the get-go. Having investigated the crime scene on the day of the bombing, Cornick was assigned to work with the Justice Department on the case. His initial reaction was, "No. I'm not. I have no intention of working with them. I don't want some assistant U.S. attorney telling me how to run a case." Gene Propper was the twenty-nine-year-old assistant U.S. Attorney assigned to lead the prosecution. Born in the Bronx, he was tall and bearded and rode a motorcycle to work. Propper had developed a reputation as a tireless and talented prosecutor, winning guilty verdicts on all but one of his fifty felony cases over a five-year period. He was brash, ambitious and had a sharp sarcastic tongue. Despite his unconventional image, Propper was apolitical, although he occasionally expressed vaguely liberal views about race and civil liberties. He knew this case was important, a career maker.

An hour after the bombing, Propper sat in the cafeteria of the federal courthouse in Washington. The U.S. attorney approached him, "Look, we've never had one like this. We may never solve it no matter what you do. Give it your best shot. It's not going to be any fun." Propper knew nothing about Chile, spoke no Spanish, and had never prosecuted a political case. But he determined this might be an opportune coda before jumping ship into the private sector. He had paid his dues and begun planning a transition to private practice, where the money was better.

"This is going to be a three-ring circus. The FBI should have jurisdiction. No doubt the CIA will stick their nose in, if it's not already there. Not to mention D.C. police," Propper complained to his new FBI partner. "How can we make sure they all don't start fighting and screw this up?" Turf wars between agencies were always a big part of the investigation terrain, particularly with such a visible crime scene in the middle of Washington D.C. Propper heard good things about Cornick, notwithstanding that he had a deep Southern drawl and talked too much. The bigger issue was the crime itself. Less than ten percent of bombing cases are ever solved as most of the evidence is instantly destroyed and almost never do the perpetrators linger at the crime scene. The bombing almost certainly was political, with foreign government involvement. Spy agencies weren't going to help. The last thing Gene Propper wanted to be was a referee – or pawn between competing government bureaucracies.

"You might as well know what you are in for," Cornick told Propper the first morning they got together. He led Propper into his small office and motioned to him to have a seat. "Gene, there are people in the U.S. government who get regular information about international assassins. I'm not just talking about the CIA either. I'm talking about the Defense Intelligence Agency, the National Security Agency, various military attaches all over the world, and the Bureau. They use this information mostly to keep track of things in case of foreign travel by high American officials. They don't want these killers near Kissinger when Kissinger goes to Paris or somewhere. Are you with me?" he paused to take a gulp of coffee and the measure of this lawyer. He sat back in his metal chair. "The first thing you've got to do is assess the veracity of the source. Is he a valid conduit? What's his track record?" Cornick was known for his loquacious stemwinders and was difficult to interrupt. "Then you've got to assess the information itself. Can it be verified? Does it contain facts that you can use for collaboration? And finally, you've got to look at where the information will take you. A lot of these leads sound sexy as hell, but they only take you about as far as the end of your thumb."

The 'Mouth of the South' was also concerned that this young energetic lawyer might get his hands on CIA material and go off in too many directions at once. Propper finally jumped in. "From what you are telling me, it sounds like we're going to need a lot of help with all this verification. How many agents do you have in Chile?"

"Only one," sighed Cornick. "We have a legat down there." *Lee-Gat.*

"Only one?" he answered. "What's a legat?"

"Legal attaché. That's the FBI representative in the embassy."

"Carter, how can we investigate Chile with only one guy?"

"That's not the half of it. That lee-gat doesn't even live in Chile. He's based in Buenos Aires. He covers Chile on road trips, but also has to cover Uruguay, Paraguay, Peru, Argentina, and maybe a few others. I don't know. But I do know that the legats have absolutely no investigative power overseas. They can't question witnesses. They can't run informants. They can't even carry their FBI credentials down there, because they don't mean anything. They have no more authority down there than any private citizen. All they could do is maintain the best possible liaison with the local law enforcement people."

"That's just terrific," Propper answered with huff. "I can't believe this. How are we supposed to do anything?"

"The guy down there is one of the best in the Bureau, Gene. And one good lee gat is worth about a dozen of those spooks you've been talking to. The Agency itself doesn't have that many people in Chile."

"Well, at least they live there," said Propper. "For God's sake, what's the legat's name?"

"Bob Scherrer."

"Do you know him?"

"No, but everyone says he's solid. He's been there six years."

Special FBI agent Robert Scherrer had been based at the U.S. Embassy in Buenos Aires since 1970. He too was a hard-driving New Yorker, raised in a lower middle class Brooklyn family of Irish and German descent. He was five-foot-five, soft-spoken with red hair, known and trusted across the continent. The FBI recruited him when he was eighteen, gave him a job as a filing clerk and sent him to Fordham University to get his law degree. Scherrer possessed terrific instincts about how this collection of countries operated. It had gotten more challenging over the past few years. These senior military guys only understood brute force and their sole agenda was to stay in power. Most were hard-headed and poorly-educated and many of their transgressions should be prosecuted at the international court at The Hague. Scherrer was a good confidante with most of the non-political bureaucrats in the different agencies who found their leaders repugnant. He knew a lot about Latin America, international investigations, and diplomacy. A growing chunk of his time over the last few years had been spent in vain liaising with local police and intelligence contacts in search of 'disappeareds' in Argentina on behalf of U.S. relatives.

Scherrer fielded cables from Washington after the Letelier bombing and went to work. He nosed around at the Argentine military intelligence services. They were a smart, collegial bunch he'd known for the past six years. "It was a wild Condor operation," one of his sources blurted out over drinks at Café Tortoni. "Those lunatics in Santiago are going to ruin everything. This will hurt us all. This is bad business – going way outside into Europe and other countries. Condor was a good operation, this will ruin it."

Scherrer noticed some of his counterparts at other tables in the cafe. This wasn't just spies blowing smoke at one another. Scherrer knew the man well and trusted his intelligence sources. *So, this operation is called Condor?* It was described as just an information exchange, 'a computer set-up in Santiago' – an interchange and storage of data on Marxist terrorists. Scherrer kept digging. His source was irate that things had gone too far. Condor was a good operation with a good objective … until people started getting killed on Embassy Row in Washington, D.C. Scherrer kept listening – these Argentines were a talkative lot. A week after the Letelier assassination, he sent a top-secret report to Washington.

September 28, 1976

Subject: Operation Condor/Possible Relation to Letelier Assassination

Operation Condor is the code name for the collection, exchange and storage of intelligence data concerning leftists, communists, and Marxists which was recently established between the cooperating services in South America in order to eliminate Marxist terrorists and their activities in the area. In addition, Operation Condor provides joint operations against terrorist targets in member countries. Chile is the center for Operation Condor, and in addition includes Argentina,

Bolivia, Paraguay and Uruguay. Brazil has also tentatively agreed to supply input for Operation Condor.

A more secret phase involves the formation of special teams from member countries to travel anywhere in the world to non-member countries to carry out sanctions, [including] assassinations against terrorists or supporters of terrorist organizations from Operation Condor member countries. For example, should a terrorist or supporter of a terrorist organization from a member country be located in a European country, a special team from Operation Condor would be dispatched to locate and surveil the target. When the location and surveillance operation has been terminated, a second team from Operation Condor would be dispatched to carry out the actual sanctions against the target.

Scherrer's sources within the Argentine intelligence services painted the picture of a reckless, impulsive but committed collection of military and security leaders intent on destroying leftists wherever they operated. He had just learned about a new plot to assassinate three 'terrorists' in Europe; two leaders of the Junta de Coordinación Revolucionaria, an Argentine socialist organization based in Paris, and Illich Ramierez Sánchez, a committed Venezuelan Marxist better known as 'Carlos the Jackal'. The mission involved several agents, including three Chileans, two Argentines and two Uruguayans who arrived in Paris in late September. Scherrer's Argentine intelligence contact was more than happy to sabotage this and future missions, after Chile 'ruined Condor' by committing such an audacious crime in Washington, D.C. The Chileans had become cocky and poked the bear. The U.S. hadn't publicly accused the Chilean government of killing Letelier, but the CIA knew DINA was behind it. Things were very complicated in a region where no one admitted to knowing anything or anybody.

A month after the bombing, the case got an unexpected breakthrough. Operating under the premise that any Chilean conspirators 'would not be dumb enough to travel on an official passport', as one FBI source put it, agents sifted through visa applications of every Chilean who entered the United States between May and September. It was tedious, dull work reviewing thousands of applications, quickly ruling out unlikely suspects, such as families on vacation. "We need to go through them all," Propper said. "We must look through the forest to find the tree, then the twig."

Cornick and Propper learned that two Chilean Army officers tried to obtain U.S. visas over the summer, using Paraguayan passports. American ambassador George Landau became suspicious after a senior Paraguayan official called to assure him that the two Chileans 'were OK.' All of it sounded strange to the veteran diplomat. Why would they travel via Asuncion? And, why would a Paraguayan vouch for two Chilean army officers? It sounded fishy. Landau took photographs of the page with the men's passport photos and sent it on to Carter Cornick in Washington. Their names were Juan Williams, 34 years old, light hair, blue eyes, 1.89 meters tall and Alejandro Romeral, 26 years old, dark hair and eyes, 1.74 meters tall. Cornick checked with the INS. There was no record of anyone with those names entering the United States. He followed up with the Miami field office. No matches. There were other more promising leads to pursue beyond two Chilean army guys.

After all, relations with Chile were good. They were excellent immediately following the 1973 coup and were again strong, after a difficult year when Pinochet reneged on a promise to let the U.N. Human Rights Commission visit Chile. Secretary of State Kissinger had paid a visit to Santiago in June. These were allies in the fight against socialism. Scherrer understood the intelligence landscape in Latin America and sympathized with their cause and situation. Everyone knew about, but still overlooked, the kidnappings and torture. These countries were reliable, strong allies against the Soviet Union. Morality was a relative term, especially if the other option was a communist continent on America's doorstep.

In early October, the *Miami Herald* received a message from a man with a Spanish accent who claimed credit for the D.C. bombing in the name of the anti-Castro movement. His name was Orlando Bosch, the banished leader of the violent terrorist organization called the Cuban National Movement, who was currently imprisoned in Venezuela after his involvement in a Cubana Airlines bombing that killed 75 people. The CIA originally recruited him for the Bay of Pigs operation, but determined he was too unpredictable to be counted on. Bosch was unapologetic about his desire to rid Cuba of Castro. From his jail cell in Caracas, he happily recounted thirty or so plots to undermine Castro's rule throughout the 1960s, including a homemade bazooka attack on a Polish freighter in Biscayne Bay. Bosch was just whacked enough to think he could pull off an assassination 1.7 miles from the White House from a jail cell in Caracas. Rumors suggested Bosch hired two Cuban brothers, Ignacio and Guillermo Novo and another CMN guy, Virgilio Paz to murder Letelier. But again no one was talking on the record, nor was there any hard evidence that would stand up in court. The anti-Castro militants still had lots of friends in the right places in the U.S. government.

The assassination of Orlando Letelier continued to be covered in *The Post*, although by late autumn, the story had fallen into a single column in the middle of the Metro section. After the initial finding that the Chilean secret police were behind the bombing, very little new evidence was turned up. There was an emerging theory about a lover's triangle, as Letelier was known to have a wandering eye. The most likely scenario remained that the Cubans did it for Pinochet. There were enough nutty anti-Castro freelancers around who would happily take out a left-leaning diplomat.

Willie's job interviews were going nowhere. He met with several of his parents' friends, ranging from a successful private banker to another real estate broker. Mr. DeCamp indicated that he could bring him on as a 'runner' in his commercial brokerage group. Everyone was polite and encouraging. *You just have to sell yourself as the most talented and hard-working candidate out there*, they told him. His parents had a few connections, although it was apparent that Willie was a lousy self-promoter. He needed to get away from home and go somewhere to figure out how to become an adult.

"Have you voted, William?" Alma started in. It was breezy and the sky was bright, a happy day to turn Gerald Ford out of office. She already cast her vote for Jimmy Carter. This was her second time voting in a U.S. election and Alma Alvarez was not going to be denied her right as a new citizen.

"Not yet," he answered shyly. Willie was half-asleep as he spread rock-hard refrigerated butter on his English muffin. He fixed a cup of coffee, but mornings for him were rarely productive. He got home from his bartending job at O'Shaunessey's after midnight and looked lost in his own kitchen.

"Well, you need to vote today," she chirped. "We've talked about this many times. Do you want me to fix you something to eat? Are you hung-over?"

"No, just tired. I promise I'll go vote this morning." Willie's hair was uncombed and he wore a wrinkled tee shirt. "I'm voting for the peanut farmer, just like we discussed," he chuckled. "He'll be better on human rights."

"The morning is half over," she answered, methodically separating the damp pile of clothes that she put into the dryer. "I voted at seven a.m. In case you forgot our talk from last week, apathy about voting is unacceptable. And Gerald Ford will only continue with the status quo with the generals."

"I will, I will, I will," he answered again, defeated. "You win."

"We all win. Remember what we talked about last week? Voting is a privilege that my sister and brother don't have anymore. Do you want a dictatorship like what we have in Uruguay? Do you want the police showing up on your doorstep and throwing you in the back of a car? That's what happens when the right to vote is taken away. I know. So, go vote! Your precinct is located at George Washington Middle School over on Mount Vernon Avenue."

While the interview process was slow going, Willie became fascinated by the primer he was receiving in Latin American politics and history from Alma. It sounded exciting and … a little dangerous. Four months ago, Willie couldn't have told you the first thing about Argentina or Uruguay. Now he, at least, could rattle off some basic facts about the continent and have a cursory political discussion about what was going on. Alma had lit a fire to his cautious imagination. News coverage of the region was scant, and no one dared write critical pieces on the 'disappearances' except Bob Cox, publisher of the *Buenos Aires Herald*, Argentina's long-standing English-language daily newspaper.

Willie devoured Alma's perspectives on everything from Uruguayan history and politics to the economic and class imbalances that were ruining the countries in the Southern Cone. He tried to converse with her in Spanish where he could. "When you come from a small place that Americans can't find on a map, you need to know about what's going on in the world. Many of us in South America have dealt with this for the past fifteen years. Our economies went to hell after World War II. The divide between the working class and landowners got worse and worse. People got mad, so the military stepped in. We have no responsible political class, or middle class for that matter.

"You should go look around for yourself. What else do you have going on?" she continued, probably with more honesty than Willie was used to. When Alma got a head of steam talking, it was time to sit back, listen and not interrupt. Willie and Alma had spent the last two months talking about his future and that was Alma's simple pitch. Travelling around South America for a few months would give him time to get away and think about what's next. It was something he couldn't discuss with his father or mother, but Beryl was all for it. Alma was right: he had nothing else to do beside pursuing jobs he wasn't interested in. Willie was already bartending a few nights a week in Old Town, just to get out of the house and make some money. Why not go to Argentina … or Uruguay? He spoke some Spanish, enough to get around … or to get something to eat.

"But you said these governments are dangerous, assassinating people in broad daylight in the middle of cities?" he asked.

"They come in the night, selectively. No one will bother you if stay away from politics. Just spend your good tourist dollars, and they'll leave you alone. Hell, they need all the hard currency they can get these days. I still have some family there. You should go."

I should go. After all, what else do I have to do? Alma's encouragement made Willie feel alive for the first time since graduation. It sounded real, far more real than selling himself, or commercial real estate.

His father was nonplussed. "So, instead of getting a job, you want to hitchhike around South America looking for meaning in life? *How do you plan to support yourself? Where do you want to live? What do you want to do?* The barrage of serious questions unnerved Willie. The answers felt so monumental that he didn't want to pick something and realize a decade later he made the wrong choice. At least Willie could go there under the premise of opening his mind. Beryl had encouraged him to get away from home. "Why do you think I went to graduate school? We all need a break between college and the real world."

Willie had heard his father's opinion on 'finding himself' before. *Look in the god-damned mirror and earn some money.* That was his opinion on new age things that came with this new generation. *We give them educations and then they want experiences.* Willie knew little about Alma's life in Uruguay, other than her family emigrated to the States eight years earlier. Economic opportunity was the reason given, although increasingly she provided Willie with more personal history. Her husband, Patricio was a civil engineer with the City of Alexandria. They were from Pando, a small town outside Montevideo that got caught in the crossfire between the government and a leftist guerrilla group in the sixties. Like everywhere, those few in the middle -- like the Álvarez's – suffered. Her family packed up and moved to Washington in 1968. Alma still had relatives in Montevideo, although things in Uruguay had gotten worse. The military seized power in 1973 and immediately began abducting young people perceived as leftist. Alma's niece Marcela and her husband Paulo were two of the 'disappeareds', although she never mentioned it to the Thomas family until now. The Letelier assassination had brought a temporary spotlight on the Southern Cone, but the event had already faded in the newspapers. Georgia governor Jimmy Carter had just been elected President and Patty Hearst was sentenced to seven years for her role in a bank robbery. South America was disappearing again into the American background.

"We'll give you a loan for the airfare," his father finally acquiesced, after strong female advocation. "The rest is on you. Go sow your oats for a few months. It'll do you some good, son. Treat Alma's family to dinner. I hear the food is wonderful." Willie knew that this whole process irritated his dad, and he was simply outnumbered. *Everyone's so easy on Willie. Heaven forbid Baby Jesus has to put a suit on like everyone else.* The idea of 'bumming around' was not an acceptable way of living to Big Bill, no matter what anyone said. But his mother, a softie who indulged her baby son when she could, and big sister prevailed. Sowing wild oats before settling down to go to work was a new twist for his father who found himself shot in the butt in a marsh near Anzio, Italy three months after his twentieth birthday.

"I'll pay you back. I promise." Willie heard that BA was a big, beautiful city with wide boulevards and handsome people. He could stay for a few months, nose around, improve his Spanish, and come home refreshed and motivated, ready to take on a serious job hunt. He was relieved his father had been agreeable, although Willie knew that he'd have limited patience if he returned without a detailed future plan.

Four

Buenos Aires, Argentina

January – March, 1977

Willie Thomas departed Dulles for Buenos Aires on January 18th, 1977. His return ticket was dated for March 15th, although the travel agent said it could be changed once he arrived. His plans were loose. He had $1800 in American Express traveler's checks tucked inside a money belt. It was three hours to Miami, and another ten to BA sitting in row 46B. The rear of the plane was empty, although the cabin air had a thick, stale smell of a crowded salon, with burnt tobacco and strong perfume. Most of the passengers were awake, talking, drinking wine and smoking cigarettes. It made Willie excited, like a child on Christmas Eve trying to close his eyes, but finding new topics to think about as he peeked out of the porthole at the dark continent below. He heard that Argentines were outgoing, friendly and loved their cafes and steaks. The best steaks in the world, reportedly. What wasn't to love about a place like that?

"You must go to La Cabaña," the older man, sharing the row of seats in the rear of the plane, implored. He introduced himself as Jorge. "The best beef in the world. *Se derrite en tu boca*; it melts in your mouth." He took another deep drag of his cigarette and gulped red wine from the plastic cup on the tray table. Jorge was small and crinkled, but had a gentleman's bearing. His threadbare Harris tweed blazer was draped across his slim crossed legs and a knotted Windsor tie was pulled up to his thin neck. Jorge's ample grey hair was slicked back off his face, highlighting his bushy, silver eyebrows. He had a worldly elegance and spoke quietly, but quickly. "The generals can't ruin our land and our cattle." Jorge explained that Argentina was undergoing a 'national reorganization process', or *'el proceso,'* a euphemism the military leaders used to describe the state-sponsored crackdown on its left-leaning citizens.

"You have Triple A in America, the automobile association," he continued quietly, sipping his wine. "Our AAA, the Alianza Anticomunista Argentina, kills our citizens." He paused. "Anyone who disagrees, *poof*, they disappear." His eyes darted around the rear cabin of the plane. It was mostly empty and he wanted to be sure. A middle-aged couple slumped on each other three rows forward, across the aisle, were snoring. Jorge's eyes grew larger as his hands became expressive, hoarsely whispering to Willie across the middle seat. Willie tried to take it all in, but he was tired and the continent below was pitch black and endless. They must be over the Amazon in Brazil, he reckoned, looking through the porthole, with no sign of civilization appearing in any direction. A well-dressed stranger on a plane, certainly no rabble rouser best he could tell, reiterated what Alma said.

"They killed a Jesuit priest and the brother of another president, last year." Jorge said as he gulped down the rest of his wine and lit another cigarette. "They say it is for our protection, that these people are Marxists." He waved his other hand dismissively. "Normal people who disagree? Isn't that why we all left Europe? To have voices and democracy. Marxists? *Pshaw*." Willie wanted to relay the story of his housekeeper's niece, but decided against it. Jorge used the Spanish word 'los desaparecidos' as though this was an army of lost people, a colony out in the pampas, waiting to be discovered and rescued.

Willie listened, nodding to help his comprehension, realizing four years of high school Spanish wasn't up to the pace of his seatmate. He picked up just enough of the key words to get the gist of the conversation. Jorge spoke in a high, excited pitch, mixing in English when Willie looked lost. Jorge talked about kids around Willie's age being abducted, drugged, and thrown out of helicopters into the ocean. He used the term *caravanas de la muerte* -- 'death caravans' -- referring to the army forces in Chile who 'helicopter-hopped' between detention facilities, selecting individuals for torture and murder. He used his index finger pointing to his head, *boom, boom*. "There are detention facilities where people are tortured and killed. We, the public, cannot know. But everyone knows. And everyone knows someone."

The youth hostel in Recoleta sat along a side street, near the cemetery. The building was a gracious old aristocrat's home that had been chopped up into smaller apartments, with shops along the street front. Buenos Aires was an elegant city, best he could tell noticing the clean, shady squares and tree-lined streets as he stared out of the rear window of the taxicab. The buildings were large and important, taking up entire city blocks. But within the elegant old bones of the city, BA appeared frayed -- its citizens still dressed well, but like Jorge, the city looked second-hand and lived in. Many of the first floors were given over to small shops, selling cheap clothes and souvenirs. It was a proud country working hard to make-do graciously. Alma gave him the telephone number of her niece Cristina, who lived in the San Telmo neighborhood. She was an architect in her late twenties, and single. A place to start, he assured his father, and of course he'd buy her dinner. The weather was warm and humid as Willie got his bearings, studying the city map. The couple running the hostel pointed out a walking route down the Avenida 9 de Julio to La Boca, returning along the Paseo Colón to Plaza de Mayo, the city's central square. "It'll take you a few hours. Unless, of course, you want to take tango lessons," he continued, smiling. "Or, stop at a café and watch people walk by. The city is good for that. And our beer is good. Quilmes." He winked.

Willie tucked his passport into his money belt and struck out along the main artery south. It reminded him of Washington with its grand thoroughfares and large stone structures and monuments. There were several large statues of heroic men on horseback dominating the plazas along his route. Willie was jet-lagged and disoriented, although the warm breeze following him down Avenida 9 de Julio caused him to quicken his pace and feel alive. *I'm finally away from home,* he celebrated with a jump to his step, *and it's summertime.* He passed buskers along the route playing guitars and bandoneons, which added to his good mood. It was nice to feel the warm breeze of summer in January. He turned left and headed over to the Plaza de Mayo. The formidable, pinkish Casa Rosada anchored the eastern end of the park. Willie noticed a small group of middle age women with signs reading 'Niños Desaparecidos' and 'Madres de Plaza de Mayo.' They were grieving as onlookers and police looked on, marching slowly around the square, chanting. The posters displayed grainy black and white photographs of young people, male and female; many didn't look old enough to be out of high school, much less be troublemakers. *Here it is again,* he thought to himself, the dirty war. Willie paused and took in the scene, thinking back to the conversation on the plane with the old man in the tweed jacket. *We, the public, cannot know. But, everyone knows. And everyone knows someone."*

The crowd of women at the square was small, perhaps two dozen. Passers-by stopped for a few seconds, then noting the uniform presence, kept walking with their eyes down and heads bowed. The mothers were despondent, some were chanting the names of children, *Ignacio, Claudia, Mateo, Joaquín,* while others cried hysterically. Most of the women wore white headscarves with names of their children embroidered in blue. Willie stared over at the police, who looked disinterested or perhaps uncomfortable on a hot day in their wool uniforms. Willie walked on, heading north toward Recoleta. He thought about what Alma said. 'We have no responsible political class, or middle class for that matter. It has been a mess for twenty years.'

Willie crossed the street and ducked into a café next to the hostel. 'Una Quilmes, por favor." The café was small with wooden paneling and a cool white tile floor. A large fan spun languidly as the waiter returned and placed the beer on the small table, smiled, then turned away with a nod. It had been a good first day, but Willie's feet were sore and he longed for a nap. He enjoyed his first walk around the city. It was clean and elegant, as advertised. Wealthy too, judging by the large buildings along his route and lack of beggars asking for money. It was far less fearsome than his hometown by a large margin. He was happy to cool his swollen feet and the Quilmes tasted particularly good.

Willie picked up the guidebook and began reading about the short-lived return of Juan Peron from twenty years in exile in Spain. Peron was a charming post-war populist who opened up the closed world of landed power to the people. He and his wife Eva became a Hollywood-style couple who fought for the poor, before the military ran them out in the early-fifties. His brand and the country's longing to recapture its glorious past lingered in the new grim world of national regeneration. Willie finished his beer, paid the waiter, and headed to the hostel. He climbed the stairs to the third floor and sat down on this bed in the large open room. There were eight single bunk beds in and his was next to the bathroom. He had met a German couple earlier in the morning who looked to be travelling for a long time, given the size of their backpacks.

Willie took off his shoes and trousers and stored them under the cot. He lay down on his sleeping bag and pulled the pillow over his head, trying to quiet his mind and fall asleep. *What am I doing here?* He wasn't exactly sure. He skimmed over the blur of events that had occurred today, trying to close his eyes and sleep. It was a beautiful city, so much more European-looking than he expected. One thing stood out -- those mothers wailing in the plaza with their signs and pictures of missing children. It was disturbing to hear about torture chambers and death caravans, but the mothers with missing children at the square were too real.

After tossing and turning for a half hour, Willie went downstairs with the slip of paper that Alma gave him: 'Cristina Alvarez, BA, 4314-3719.' The hostel owner smiled and pointed to the telephone in the small office behind the creaky stairway. Alma said very little to Willie about Cristina, except that she was smart. "An architect in Buenos Aires who started in little Uruguay. You should look her up. She was just a teenager when we left."

"Cristina?" he replied, after she answered the telephone. "This is William Thomas. Your aunt Alma suggested I call you. I'm in Buenos Aires. Is now a good time to speak?"

"Oh, hello. Nice to hear from you. My auntie wrote to say you might call. Right now, is difficult," she said in flawless English. "But, how about dinner one night later this week? I have a big client meeting tomorrow."

It was late when Cristina came into the bar at La Cabaña. Willie checked his watch. 10:15. They agreed to meet at 10. *These Argentines do eat late.* He had finally adjusted to the rhythm of South American dining. It was Friday night and Willie enjoyed the parade of handsome people sitting importantly at the tables. Their clothes were finely made, but shop worn, like the old man on the airplane. The room was large and elegant, but had to begun to show its age. Faded old world elegance in the new world, he laughed. D.C. was far worse -- there was no style to begin with.

Cristina Alvarez turned a few of the older gentlemen's heads as she passed by the huge stuffed cow guarding the entrance into the restaurant. She was slight with medium-length dark wavy hair but walked with a confident stride. She wore a stylish black tunic top and jeans. Willie stood up from his stool pleased, as she extended her hand. "You must be William?"

"Willie, por favor," he answered somewhat awkwardly, shaking her firm hand. He had noticed a woman walking into the restaurant and hoped she was Cristina. "It's nice to meet you. Thank you for coming. Please have a seat, our table's almost ready."

"I couldn't resist the invitation. Poor architects can't afford to come here," she quipped, climbing onto the stool, looking around the restaurant.

Willie smiled at the introduction, taking in this new person as the maître d arrived with menus to show them to their table. "This is the one restaurant I was told to come to. My seatmate on the flight raved about it." Willie looked around the elegant room filled with busy men in white jackets darting between tables. "How long has this restaurant been around?"

"Forever," she answered, as they were seated at a small table, back near the kitchen. "I think it started before the second World War. I know De Gaulle and Walt Disney ate here. As did Henry Kissinger, just last year. There are photographs of them in the entry." She smiled playfully. An older man in a white jacket arrived and poured water into their glasses.

"He was probably with General Videla celebrating their support for the war against the Marxists," Willie answered. He had tracked down several newspaper and *Time* Magazine articles at the library, but mostly he listened closely, and repeatedly, to Alma's opinionated view of post-war South American politics.

"My auntie didn't tell me you knew about our politics, but yes, this is where important people meet and eat." She smiled at the rhyme. "Welcome to our city of good air, such as it is these days." Willie again looked out over the large festive room and opened the menu.

"I looked for a good travel guide for you," Cristina continued, reaching down to her handbag. "The best I could find in English is this one," she said, handing a wrapped parcel to Willie. "How long are you here?"

"A few months. I wanted to look around, see the country. I've never been to South America."

"You're like most Americans. They've heard of Machu Picchu, Rio, and the Amazon River, but little else. Do American children learn anything about South America in school?"

"No. I didn't. Americans know very little about the world outside America … or outside their hometown." He shrugged with a slight smile.

Cristina nodded in disappointment. "You should travel around and see Argentina. It's beautiful. But fucked up." She smiled. "Particularly now."

Willie looked over at Cristina. He wasn't used to a woman saying 'fucked up.' He'd heard South American women were polite and more conservative than Americans. Cristina's black tunic shirt, thick wavy hair and denim jeans cast her quite differently. "Tell me about your family. Your aunt got me to take notice of this part of the world." At this point, the stout waiter who had drawn this young, budget-conscious couple arrived ready to take their order.

"Not a pretty picture, but let's order first. *Bife de Lomo* is what you call a tenderloin. Much in this country is overrated. That is one thing that is not."

Despite his concern about being overheard, Willie and Cristina spent a good part of dinner talking about Orlando Letelier's' murder, pausing with smiles as waiters and other patrons walked by to the kitchen or washroom. "It happened here, too. They murdered a Chilean general the same way, with a car bomb. They shot and killed two Uruguayan MPs, and the ex-president of Bolivia in the last year. One of the MPs was a family friend."

Willie was anxious having this conversation in such a public place, although Cristina didn't appear concerned. She continued in English. "Most of these military people are stupid. They have no education; they know power, that's all. It's all about kissing the right ass. My grandparents got on the wrong side of them. Most of us stayed, Alma's family left."

"What do you mean, *the wrong side?*"

"There was a group in Uruguay called the Tupamaros." Cristina took a long sip from her glass of wine and continued. "Very left wing and militant. At first, they were liked. They were like Robin Hood; steal from the rich, give to the poor. Then they started kidnapping and killing people. The saddest part of this is my sister is an artist. She couldn't hurt a flea and doesn't know one political party from another." Cristina barely touched her meal as she talked, sometimes fluently, other times haltingly. "We haven't seen her in five months. She and her husband were rounded up. And she was pregnant."

"Rounded up? And, taken where?"

"No one knows. My parents hired someone to find her, but they're still looking. There's an old garage on the outskirts of the city where many people have been taken and tortured. A few get released, most do not." Cristina moving hands suddenly rested and she exhaled. "It's not like you can call the police." She sat back in her chair, shoulders slumped, emotional energy expended. She looked across at Willie, regaining a slight shy smile.

"I'm so sorry. I can't imagine." Willie felt the urge to help, but didn't know where to begin. The concept of disappearances was so alien. How could it happen to just normal middle class people? How do you live every day knowing your sister may be dead or tortured? This conversation made him think about his own sister, the brightest and most competent person he knew, just one day disappearing into thin air without a trace. What an existence to suffer through every day, not knowing if you too are on a list. The military were list keepers. "So, do you have any leads?" Willie didn't really know what else to say, although he knew it made him sound stupid.

"There are places all around you hear about. They might be in the apartment building across the street. Or it might be an old military barracks or an *estancia* in the country? Who knows?" Cristina sounded weary. "We just hope they are alive. Have you read the Amnesty International report? It's pretty damning."

Willie shook his head, remembering Alma's remark about her outspoken niece, the successful architect. "We're doing all we can," she continued. "As I said, it's not like we can report anything to the police. Hope and prayer are nice things to say, but neither will get them back. We all feel useless. I refuse to accept that she and Paulo are dead. Marcela was pregnant too." Cristina was drained from the conversation, but her damp eyes still sparkled.

"Let's talk about something else. So, when are you going to Montevideo? Auntie said you wanted to look around, before you headed south."

"What's there to do in Montevideo?"

"Nothing. It's a nice quiet city, worth a few days. Not much more," she snickered. "The old city is small, and very manageable to walk around. There are nice beaches too. We still have family there. My brother Ricardo would be happy to show you around," she smiled impishly. "That is, if you call him after noon. He's the fun one in the family. I'm teased as the serious responsible one, the nerdy architect. Marcela is the artist, the one of us who smells the flowers and wouldn't hurt a flea. Ricardo is a charmer, and not like any of us. He's a sweet boy who loves life. As you've witnessed, I'm not particularly sweet and life's not great."

La Cabaña was still bright and busy at quarter to twelve. Willie had pumped himself full of coffee as they talked through the evening. Mostly Cristina talked and he listened. He was trying to sort out all that he had been hearing for two-and-half hours. A beautiful Argentine architect was sharing her family's tragedy with him. He wanted so much to help, but knew listening was the only contribution this evening. "Would you care for anything else? Unlike me, you have to work tomorrow. This has been fun." Fun was not the word he had in mind, but it still popped out of his mouth.

Cristina smiled and nodded, looking at her watch. "It is late, sorry I talked all night. The past six months have been difficult. I think about my sister every day, but I can't call the police. Or maybe they will throw me in the back of an old Ford? Or kidnap me, give me a shot of sodium pentothal and toss me out of a helicopter. It's a strange time in Argentina."

They walked slowly toward her apartment in San Telmo. Willie wanted to take her arm, but felt awkward and intimidated. Their dinner was so honest and revealing and they talked as new, excited acquaintances sometimes do, full of honesty and personal details without any expectation of a continued relationship. Cristina shared a little about her architecture projects. She recently designed a block of apartments that would be built right down at the docks at Puerto Madero.

The city was grand and quiet at midnight, with only an occasional taxi cab slowing, then continuing on. A warm breeze blew at their backs as they walked toward her apartment. "You should definitely go to Bariloche. It's our little piece of Switzerland with chocolate and Saint Bernard dogs. You might even run into Joseph Mengele. The 'Angel of Death' lives there quite openly. I'm not joking. I told you this country is fucked up."

They turned onto Paseo Colón and Willie was surprised to see small cafes still open. Cristina turned to him as she located keys in her purse. "I want to thank you for dinner. And, thank you for listening to me. I hope I didn't seem like a deranged basket case. I'm really quite a normal and sane person."

Willie smiled awkwardly, not sure how to say goodbye. "I enjoyed the evening very much." He turned to offer his hands, smiling and Cristina grabbed him around his shoulders and squeezed him. "No, thank you William. You are the first person other than my family and my boss who knows about this. I had to tell someone. I hope it is OK." Her twinkly gaze and crooked smile disappeared as she pushed her hair back and wiped tears from her eyes. Cristina turned to unlock the front door of the apartment building, "Do call my brother. He's more fun than me." She gently pulled the front door shut and walked up the stair.

Willie lay on his bed at the hostel, thinking about the evening with Cristina. He couldn't imagine his friends being rounded up and carted away for supporting a Democrat. It was good that Jimmy Carter won. He already made human rights a big issue in the presidential campaign. Kissinger had allowed Pinochet to literally get away with murder, over and over. Cristina talked about the torture centers and confirmed the stories about airplanes dropping kids into the Rio Plata. He was intrigued by the wild and remote quality of this part of the world and by the brutality of the stories.

Montevideo and Pocitos Beach, Uruguay

Alma Ramirez could be forgiven for her exaggerated pride about her motherland. Its success – and existence -- was a secret from the world. As early as 1915, there were

laws in Uruguay for a forty-hour work week, holidays with
pay, old-age pensions, free medical care, legalized divorce,
and the nationalization of essential industries and services,
like electricity, telephones, transport, and financial services.
Capital punishment and bullfighting were outlawed and the
Church disestablished. At one point, Uruguay exported
more beef than Argentina, despite being sixteen times
smaller in size.

But Uruguay faced structural challenges, with only 500
families controlling the land and capital. Jobs in meat
processing and textiles declined after World War II and by
the early-1960s, the country's economy was in tatters. Latin
America's first urban guerrilla organization called the
Tupamaros was formed, leading the conservative
government to suspend civil liberties. Congress closed,
labor and student organizations were outlawed, and over
5000 opponents of the regime were thrown into prison.

Cristina was dismissive of Montevideo as a sleepy
inbred backwater that she was glad to move away from, but
Willie liked its smaller scale and friendliness. Cristina put
Willie in touch with her younger brother. Ricardo lived
along the Rambla in Pocitos Beach, a resort town ten miles
east of Montevideo. The city was wealthy and white, more
so than even Buenos Aires, 130 miles to the west across the
Rio Plata. The shantytowns and *favelas* that had taken root
around the edges of Caracas, Sao Paulo, Rio, and Lima
were absent here.

Willie instantly liked Ricardo. They, it turns out, were
very similar – the youngest and only sons with unsettled
career plans and overachieving older sisters. Ricardo's

talented sisters had moved to BA to pursue their creative passions. Marcela was a studio art major, who married an older graduate student after university in Cordoba. They were abducted from their apartment in Buenos Aires. Cristina was the serious middle child, getting two architecture degrees and now she worked for a respected firm in Buenos Aires. They were the ambitious ones in the family. Ricardo talked about opening a bar in Punta del Este with two friends, but the plan bounced around, with little action. Her brother was a big talker, but follow through was always his challenge.

"He's everyone's friend," she had said, somewhat derogatorily over dinner. "Never worked a full eight-hour day in his life. He's the dreamer in the family. Bless him." Ricardo, it turns out, was also the dresser in the family. He met Willie at the bus station at Plaza Cagancha and immediately took him to lunch. Ricardo was short, but handsome with a mop of dark hair and a moustache. He wore blue and red paisley slacks with a large white belt. He walked with a distinctive strut, head held high, never really looking at the pavement below his feet, like the movie was playing in his head. Ricardo wore a cream-colored rayon shirt, and a kerchief tied jauntily around his neck. They walked toward his favorite restaurant, called Soko's on Avenida 18 de Julio and took a table outside on the plaza. The waiter waved and immediately brought menus to the table. There was a thespian quality to Ricardo, part peacock, part tour guide that instantly made Willie relax.

"Everything here is delicious. Omelets, pizza, and really good lasagna. You can't go wrong. After all, half this country comes from Italy. Try Pilsen. Most like your Budweiser." The waiter smiled.

Ricardo was comfortable in his own skin and clearly knew his way around the watering holes of the city. He also talked a lot about women, nodding and pointing out attractive pedestrians strolling around the main square. "So, Cristina tells me you just finished university and are exploring South America? Good for you. Americans hardly ever come here. We're like Canada, the dull neighbor next door."

Willie smiled and after a clink of glasses, gulped down half of his beer and looked at the menu. His sister had made the same comparison. He quickly scanned the menu. "I'll try the lasagna and a small salad," he said, handing the menu back to the waiter. "Thank you for reaching out. What should I see?"

'Well," Ricardo replied, "There's not that much to see. We can go to the Gaucho museum which is interesting, but dull. It'll take fifteen minutes, although the belts they sell in the gift shop are worth buying. Tonight, I'll show you the fun Uruguay. Lots of bars, discotheques and pretty girls." He raised his eyebrows. "Just east of here," he said pointing out to the horizon over his shoulder.

Willie remembered Cristina's words of warning about her party-boy brother. But if he was being honest, Willie was itching to have a big night on the town. "Be careful, he'll keep you up all night," she cautioned. "He likes discos and girls." Willie looked forward to this change of venue, behavior and new company. He spent most of his time in

Buenos Aires alone, sightseeing, exploring, and practicing his Spanish. He ate dinner at a fancy steak house, but mostly he dined alone in inexpensive cafes near the hostel. His Spanish was barely passable, and he didn't have a clue where to begin with Argentine women. Cristina was certainly attractive, but she scared him to death. She was a serious person and a few years older, and they had serious conversations about torture and rape. Not exactly the language of flirtation. Cristina just seemed a lot older and wiser. He thought of his sister Beryl again as the waiter delivered a towering serving of lasagna.

"You won't starve here." Ricardo quickly waved toward the empty beer glasses and smiled happily as steam rose from the plate. There was enough food to feed four people.

"So, Cristina tells me your sister disappeared five months ago. Have you had any contact at all?" Willie didn't want to jump into the deep end of family affairs with a complete stranger, but he knew it would come up over his two weeks here. They might as well deal with it right away.

Ricardo's salesman smile drooped behind his moustache. "No Willie, I have not. The family tried to make contact, but we don't know where she is. I personally stay the hell out of politics. It's crazy around here. They knock down doors of houses with the wrong address. Then they realize they fucked up and took the wrong person. But letting them go is more trouble than it's worth. There would be investigations and it's just easier if they disappear in the night and are tossed away. No trial, no nothing. It's really fucked up."

"Your sister mentioned a garage in BA. Something Olivetti, like the typewriter," Willie continued.

"Close. It's called Automotores *Orletti*, out near the airport. There are some gruesome stories coming out of there that get me *real jumpy*." Ricardo withdrew into his chair with a grimace. "My family's name is on some lists for no good reason. It's fucked up."

"That's what I hear, too. Innocent students being kidnapped in the night. I noticed some women at the big square in the city. They were marching around in a circle with posters of their children. It was unsettling."

"That's why I stay out of politics," Ricardo answered, leaning forward in his chair, tamping his cigarette out. "The police here will grab you in a second if they think you're a leftist. I keep my nose clean, sort of," he smiled. He looked around amused, and finished his beer.

Keeping his nose clean turned out to be a broken promise that evening. After lunch, a city sightseeing tour, and a shower at Ricardo's apartment, they hailed a taxi and headed east to the beach, a ten-minute drive. Willie liked being clean, dressed up, and out for the night in a foreign country. The surprising offer of cocaine and a joint set the tone for the evening. "We are going to the Disco-Bar," Ricardo said. "Right off the beach road. There's no cover charge and they have a band tonight. Last week, they had a magician and a strip show," he laughed. "One needs to be inventive in the entertainment business."

Ricardo had changed into a new outfit for the evening – a pair of high-waisted tan Haggar slacks and an open floral shirt. Willie wore the same button-down collared blue shirt and khaki pants he wore at La Cabaña. This was the first time in nearly a year he had gone out to a disco. 'Shake, Shake, Shake' came over the radio in the taxi and Ricardo led the band from the front seat. The older taxi driver looked puzzled, but smiled at his two musically-spirited passengers. Willie looked out the back seat window at the sweep of sand and glistening lights over the expanse of the Rio Plata. *Hard to believe that's a river,* he smiled. He was happy and hopeful and high.

The Disco-Bar was packed and lively. Willie tried to take it all in. The cover band was playing 'Brick House' as they entered. It wasn't clear the band knew the words, besides 'she's a brick house, she's mighty-mighty, built like an Amazon.' There was a group of Korean seamen from a British merchant ship playing a drinking game at a corner table. It appeared they had been at it for a while. Two bored women in two-piece bathing suits took turns on a small stage hopping up on an enormous pole, twisting themselves like pretzels. There were a smattering of other women, a few earnestly dressed for a big night out stirred their drinks at tables, while others, less concerned, danced barefoot to the band in skimpy tops. An enormous strobe light pulsed over the floor, as the DJ kept announcing 'let's go, daddy-o' to the crowd.

Willie continued sipping a beer, as Ricardo chatted with one of the owners, an older heavy-set man in high-waisted slacks and a gold chain that peeked through chest hair and open shirt. Juan, as he was introduced, looked coked up, judging by his rapid speech, grinding teeth and runny nose. Willie hoped he might have a little more to share.

"Enjoying Montevideo?" Juan asked. His English was okay, but Willie couldn't hear him over the band, who now were playing 'Best of My Love.' "First time in Uruguay?" Willie nodded cheerfully, lost in the weirdness that was the Disco-Bar. A few other scantily-dressed ladies turned their attention to the table of Korean seamen. Their eyes were glazed from the drinking game and they had silly smiles from chugging boilermakers. No one seemed to be the slightest bit concerned with their passed out friend in the corner. Willie looked over at Ricardo, who had caught his attention with a subtle touch of his right nostril.

"Did you know Uruguay was the richest country on Earth?" Juan asked, after chopping up and cutting three long lines on a framed photograph of himself he'd taken off the wall of his office. The dimly-lit room was filled with piles of receipts and invoices, two empty Pilsen kegs and merchandising posters. Several old unread copies of *El Pais*, the daily newspaper, sat on a table along with a pile of unopened mail. Willie could hear the lead singer introducing a new song in Spanish as the band broke into 'Car Wash.'

"I didn't," Willie answered. "When was that?"

"1870," he laughed. "Uruguay is small and doesn't have all the problems bigger countries have. And, most of the population is European by heritage. We never massacred Indians, like our neighbors. We won the first

World Cup ever played. We live in a very civilized place," he proudly concluded, after sucking a huge line up his nose.

Santiago, Chile

January, 1977

Michael Townley always prided himself as a nerd. He was a tall, gawky fourteen-year-old when his family moved from Waterloo, Iowa to Chile in 1957. His father was the general manager at the Ford Motor plant outside Santiago. The Townley's lived in a spacious house in the city's exclusive Providencia district and blended into the ex-pat community that made up Santiago's thin upper crust. Never a student, Townley filled his room with tools, electronics, gadgets, old radios and clocks, before dropping out of high school. Like nearly everyone in the business community, his overbearing father was concerned about the rise of Salvador Allende and the emerging labor union movement. Whether it was his father's influence, or his own evolving political beliefs, Michael Townley became a reliable assassin for Chile's intelligence service by 1974, taking out General Carlos Prats, the army commander-in-chief in Buenos Aires and Bernardo Leighton, the exiled Christian Democrat party leader in Rome in 1975.

Townley had given little thought to the Letelier mission since he returned. His DINA co-workers assured him that the Paraguayan fiasco was past; that two other men using the names of Romeral and Williams travelled to the U.S. to clean up the operation. From what he could tell in the papers, the American investigation of the murders focused on the Cubans. They had been unable to tie the bombing to either Chile or DINA. The Cubans were crazy as hell, but they never blabbed.

Townley's work with DINA had changed after Manuel Contreras' resignation. He considered himself lucky not to have been purged with many other civilian agents. The Letelier mission went as well as could be expected, although the death of the American woman was unfortunate. Operation Condor was kaput now. The European missions were terminated too. Michael Townley needed to make some money. He poured over technical handbooks and learned to write computer code with the same zeal that he brought to terrorism and bomb making. Already, he established contacts with two computer supply firms in the U.S. on behalf of DINA and a growing private corporate client list. A good portion of his basement on Lo Curro hill outside Santiago was turned into a home electronics lab, as Townley taught himself computer technology.

In late January as he and his family were packing to go on summer holiday in the south, Townley received a call from 'Fernando' in Miami. He recognized the voice as Guillermo Novo. Since the assassination, Novo was questioned several times, held and released. He was now hiding out in Little Havana wearing a wig. His voice was shrill and he spoke quickly.

"I'm sorry amigo to call, but I need a favor." Novo was breathless and he sounded desperate, forgoing the usual pleasantries around family that accompany every encounter. "I need a loan of $25,000. This case has gotten too hot, and the organization needs money to relocate some members."

Townley was sympathetic. The Cubans had been the sole focus of the investigation for six months, but had kept their mouths shut. "I understand amigo and I will pass your request on to my superiors."

That wasn't what Guil Novo wanted to hear. "It is a matter of honor and friendship between us and between our respective organizations who have shared the same values and priorities. I would hate for our partnership suffer the consequences if we are not reimbursed," Novo answered, his anger welling up.

"Of course, I understand. I will contact my superiors," Townley answered. He knew that that this type of request should be handled in person, but Manuel Contreras was on holiday fishing down the coast. There was no sense in bothering him, but he owed Novo a quick answer. He dialed a number he'd been given in case of emergencies and after several minutes of waiting, Contreras came on the line.

"I'm sorry to bother you on holiday, sir," Townley began, "but this is a unique request that needs your direction."

The line was silent for several seconds. "What is it?" he answered, impatiently.

"Our partners are seeking additional support for the mission."

"What is the status of the mission?" Contreras asked.

"It's very unlikely that the FBI has developed a strong case against the Cubans. One CNM member has been in and out of custody for six months for refusing to testify to the grand jury. The United States authorities have been unable to charge him with a crime. Another member has been living in Miami one step ahead of the police for three months. They are seeking $25,000 in additional funds."

Contreras nodded, with a scowl as the amount was revealed. He stood up and walked along the wooden deck that looked out on the churning Pacific Ocean. "I'm sorry, no money," he answered. "They can send their families to Chile to live if they want, and they will be taken care of. But the members of the team will have to fend for themselves. We no longer have that kind of budget to spend."

Townley knew that Contreras would answer that way. "I understand sir, but I think this is a good investment to ensure our partners remain silent about the activities. They have been quiet so far, despite personal risk and discomfort."

Contreras was impatient. "Are there any other subjects of urgency that you would like to discuss?"

"Well sir, if you cannot command that kind of budget yourself," Townley began in a last ditch effort. "Couldn't you ... you know ... go up higher?"

"I cannot. No one above me knows about this operation. I can't ask for money."

Five

Washington, D.C.

January - August, 1977

November's U.S. presidential election brought about a change in attitude toward the embrace of conservative dictatorships in South America. The acceptance of a neighborly bulwark against communism had come with little questioning into methods and practices. The initial government reaction to Orlando Letelier's assassination was muddled and secretive, no doubt driven by concerns of American support for, and passive involvement in, Operation Condor.

"I notice that President Ford didn't comment on the prisons in Chile," Carter probed in one presidential debate. "This is a typical example, among others, that his administration helped overthrow an elected government and helped establish a military dictatorship." Jimmy Carter ran a very different campaign than his predecessors.

Several months into the investigation of Orlando Letelier's assassination, there was little hard evidence that Gene Propper, Robert Scherrer and Carter Cornick could build a case around. The two Cuban exile brothers refused to talk and didn't seem to mind stints in jail. No one could find Virgilio Paz who vanished into thin air after the hit. He was rumored to be in Miami. Their connections to Chile's DINA and other secret police organizations were loosely made, but there was no direct evidence. The initial excitement over quickly solving the case waned and new information was picked over carefully. The U.S. government could not infer that a head of state – and a close ally – had anything to do with these murders without overwhelming evidence. More importantly, Scherrer warned his colleagues that any sign the investigation was zeroing in on Chilean suspects would cause sources to 'dry up.' There were a slew of rumors, nearly all of them pointing to an international plot to murder the left-leaning politician. Gene Propper and Carter Cornick subpoenaed the Cuban exiles in February, even offering immunity in exchange for testifying. Both declined.

Iggie Novo was dismissive. "And, so what? Let them investigate. From Washington they already sent me two appearance requests for testimony in front of a congressional commission. That doesn't worry me. They make a big noise and then they quiet down."

Cornick directed the next question at his brother. "Are you going to deny your participation in terrorist activities?"

"I have never thought of doing that," Guil answered. "But why are you staring at me? Do you think terrorists have fangs sticking out, hair standing on end, and blood on their hands?" Novo answered 104 of the grand jury's questions, dismissing it as 'a fishing expedition.' In April, he showed up again in front of another grand jury. "You are wasting taxpayer money on this. I have nothing else to say on the matter."

Meanwhile, Robert Scherrer interviewed Manuel Contreras, the Chilean head of DINA. All Contreras offered was 'confidential information' that Michael Moffit probably killed Orlando Letelier since his wife Ronni was one of Letelier's lovers. "Why else would a man sit in the back seat while a woman sat in the front?" he asked. "Michael Moffit was a cuckold."

In early May, the team got its first break in the case. A thirty-five year old Cuban exile named Ricardo Canete was arrested in New York City for passing a bad check. At the station, a veteran desk sergeant recognized Canete from previous forgery arrests and searched him. They found several marijuana joints in his pocket, a roll of counterfeit twenty-dollar bills in his wallet, and a small handgun in his crotch. He also was carrying a false New Jersey driver's license.

"Ricky, we can do this the easy way, or we can do it the hard way," the sergeant said, "and I think you're the kind of person who will want things easy." As a founding member of the Cuban Nationalist Movement, Canete knew most of the exiles, but he limited himself now to small-time forgery and counterfeiting. He was given a simple option by the NYPD: answer the FBI's questions honestly, or go to jail.

Propper and Cornick were immediately alerted to this suspicious Cuban counterfeiter who confirmed his past involvement with the CNM, but professed no knowledge of its current activities. The Cuban exile community was large; nearly all were virulently anti-Castro, but just a few were crazy enough to resort to violence. Canete was bound to know some names and he had no interest in spending a few years in a U.S. prison on weapons and counterfeiting charges. That afternoon, Cornick walked into the Lower Manhattan police station to meet with Ricardo Canete.

"Nice to meet you, Ricky. I hear you've been in touch with Iggie Novo."

Canete was wearing a suit with an open-collared dress shirt. He was in his mid-thirties, handsome with an athletic build. His English was Americanized and he spoke Spanish with the accent of his native Cuba. "That's true. I've seen a lot of him the past couple of weeks. He seems to have something on his mind."

"Look Ricky, " Cornick said. "We have reason to believe the Novo brothers might have been involved with Letelier. That's big stuff. Two homicides. If you can help me either prove it or disprove it, I'll try to help you."

Canete looked sick. "I'd really like to help you. But not on this. Not on those guys. You don't know them the way I do. They're too dangerous, way too dangerous. I don't want to get involved."

"Ricky, I'll be honest with you," Cornick leaned in. "I've had a lot of Cubans tell me, 'Fuck that Letelier. He was a Commie and I'm glad he's dead.' But I don't look at it that way. Whoever did this, murdered those people in cold blood, with a bomb. That's a chicken shit way to do things."

"Well, I agree with you on that."

"All right then," Cornick nodded. "We're finally making some progress." He paused. "Do you want something to drink? It's hot in here."

Canete shook his head.

"You think Iggie and his brother are capable of something like that?"

"Sure, they are. They've been working up to it for years," Canete answered, surprising them. "I never thought it would get this heavy, I swear to God. But I was with them last week, and Guil told me he built the bomb that blew Letelier away."

"What? Don't fuck with us about something like this," Cornick answered. *The bomb that blew Letelier away. Did he just say that?* "Hold on," he interjected, "start over, I'm going to record this. Now go back over the conversation sentence by sentence, as you remember it. Calm down. You're doing the right thing."

"If I tell you what went down, you have to protect me. Keep those crazy guys away. Send me to fuckin' Montana."

"We'll look after you, Mr. Canete ... if your story holds up." Cornick leaned across the table and pressed the record button on the cassette player.

Canete began. "I went over to meet them at the Ford dealership where Iggie works. I'd made some documents for them. He closes the place up when I get there – it's late, he's got keys to the place. We get in his car and go get a drink at a restaurant. I notice a briefcase on the front seat. It has two manila folders, one says 'Orlando Letelier' and the other says 'Chile." At the restaurant, he's real polite, asks me if I want a drink or whatever while he goes to make some calls. I have a lemon Coke.

"Then we go back to the car dealership. I need a typewriter to fill out the documents I'd brought to them. I'm typing away and Iggie wants to bullshit, you know? I began to make up a set of IDs for them. I'm bragging about my work – you know, to fill out those Army discharge ID cards, you have to know all those U.S. Army codings in your head. One mistake and you're dead, it's no good.

"And Guil says, 'I'm pretty good at my work, too,' and then he starts to brag about making bombs. He said he once made one out of a flower pot. I didn't believe him. I didn't want to be bothered by all his bullshit. So, I'm typing away. 'Sure, Guil, whatever you say.

"And, then he says, "I'm not kidding. I'm serious, my latest bomb I built was a beautiful thing, even the professionals admired it.

"Yeah, yeah," I answer, still typing away. "I'm almost finished." Then he says to me, 'Look, I made the Letelier bomb. Made it right here. Used C-4 plastic explosives because they are easiest to mold and they can produce the necessary amount of heat I needed. I used a clock with a backup acid device. Just to make sure.

"So, I said to him, 'I'm fucking impressed, Guil. But anybody can build a bomb. That was a car bomb, right? Did you have the balls to put the bomb under the car?"

"Well, I could have done it, but I didn't handle that part. A Chilean did. Tall, blond guy. I never met him before. He was hanging around, but didn't introduce himself. Probably DINA. Those fuckers are loco."

"That was it," Canete closed, sounding relieved. "I didn't know what to make of it. You know Cubans love to hear themselves talk, so I didn't know if it was true. He practically confessed to me. Macho dumbass bragging about that murder."

"Holy shit. Will you take a lie detector test?"

"Sure. Will you drop the counterfeiting charges? And protect me from those assholes? I got out of the CNM because of people like that. They're completely nuts. I don't want any more of this stuff. You gotta protect me. Fuck 'yea I'll talk. Montana? You bet. Gimme a horse and I'll disappear."

Carter Cornick stared over at his star witness, holding in a desire to give him a hug. It had been a long, slow slog to get this far. This was their first break in nine months. Canete passed his polygraph test the following week. He also noted that the photograph of 'Juan Williams' – the Chilean military officer who tried to secure a U.S. visa last summer through the Paraguayan Embassy -- bore a 'fair resemblance' to the tall, blond Chilean he saw him from a distance that night at the garage. He sure as hell didn't look Cuban.

From Buenos Aires, Bob Scherrer followed up on recurring rumors that DINA had a 'tall blond agent who looked American.' He instantly remembered the strange request last summer through the Paraguayan Embassy to admit two Chilean military officers. *One of them had an American name, something Williams.* There was a photo in the file that he sent along to Langley last summer. But he never heard back, so he hadn't thought of it since then. Scherrer flew to Santiago and spent three days poring over 1500 cards of U.S. citizens registered in Chile, who travelled to the U.S. between June and September, last year. Each one was compared to the composite sketch, built on Canete's description of the American and the visa application photograph of Chilean Captain Juan Williams. Seven men vaguely fit the description: fair-haired, early to mid-thirties. They all had Spanish surnames. But no one had any connection to the Chilean government or the intelligence community. The glimmer of hope and momentum faded. If Juan Williams was out there, he covered his tracks well. Despite the latest promising leads, what the *Washington Post* called 'one of the most complicated investigations since Watergate' was stalled, again.

Alexandria, VA

Willie Thomas, too, had hit a dry spot. His two-and-a-half months in Argentina and Uruguay awoke him to a world he didn't know existed. He had met Alma's niece and nephew. Cristina was serious and tough-minded; her brother Ricardo was anything but. It was reassuring to discover that he wasn't the only black sheep with an unsettled career path and an overachieving big sister. Cristina had showed him around BA, introduced him to family in Uruguay, and stirred him up. She was just three years older, but she already had lived a fuller life than he likely ever would. He couldn't imagine having his sister just 'disappear' into thin air.

"Why don't you write this down? Write a book. Write an article. Something," Alma dismissively suggested, after listening to Willie's series of epiphanies. She was right, again. He should write everything down, while the trip was fresh.

"Life in Uruguay during my childhood was idyllic," Alma had recalled to Willie last year. "We were an export country. We fed the world during World War II and clothed soldiers in the Korean War. Wool prices tripled and demand for uniforms surged. We had social programs for the poor; the best in South America. Then exports slowed, money dried up and unrest began. My family owned a small *estancia*. We were livestock farmers and we took care of our workers, even as the economy got worse. Once the Tupamaros came in, everything collapsed."

Willie enjoyed his Monday exchanges with Alma since he returned. With his parents both at work during the day, they talked for hours and their conversations had little to do with his professional future. Other than his sister in New York, Willie didn't have anyone else. Nearly a year after graduation, his college friends had scattered to big cities on the east coast or headed out west. Listening to Alma talk about her life mesmerized him. There was vitality and realness in her stories, a life and death quality that Americans never hear about, much less face. She enjoyed a brief period of privilege when her family fed the world and world leaders at La Cabaña. Her childhood was a time of happiness, family and love for her country and its fertile land. And then it came crashing down. The economy went first. Politicians tried to fix it and were thrown out. Now the military were taking their shot. Willie admired Alma's defiance and activism for her homeland.

Alma regaled Willie with stories of growing up in Pando with an enormous family, all close but going in different directions. Coming from a small family with a distant but demanding father, Willie loved her tales of mischief and Sunday *asados*, where anywhere from ten to twenty relatives would show up. Alma painted the picture of a moveable feast, with children and grandparents alike simply enjoying one another. All they ever had to do was throw another steer on the *parilla*. She talked about Marcela, Ricardo and Cristina and they laughed about Ricardo's penchant for snappy clothes and his confident gait even as a boy. "He always walked into rooms like he owned them. He talked about the latest news from abroad, even though he'd never left Uruguay," Alma laughed. They joked about how different he and Cristina were, she with the serious, nodding gaze and assertive left hand that put things in order. Marcela was the oldest by a few years and was the gentle soul of the family. Like all of the Alvarez family, she was talented, but tough and practical too.

Alma continued to pass along salacious stories to Willie about what the military governments were doing to its citizens. The most recent Amnesty International report, which he picked up and read closely after Cristina mentioned it at La Cabaña, detailed pages after pages of names of young men and women who were arrested and detained.

"… Alicia Carlota Marambo was imprisoned for three years. She did not know what allegations there were against her, but she had been held under Law 2023 as a 'highly dangerous' prisoner … "

"… Ana Inez Gonzales was arrested on 7 February 1975 and had been in this cell for the past eleven months. She was first abducted from a street in San Justo and taken to the Villa Devoto, where she was subjected to electric shock treatments, repeated blows, and rape. She also had to watch her husband being tortured. She had been charged with 'illicit association', but she did not know what association she was alleged to have conspired … "

" … Margarita Juana Hobson was arrested in a car with her boyfriend on 20 May 1976. They were both taken to a facility in Buenos Aires, where she was blindfolded and maltreated. She preferred not to describe in detail what happened to her. She does not know what happened to her boyfriend. She was accused of being in possession of arms, but she did not know who was supposed to be investigating the case and she had not seen her lawyer in over a month and a half ..."

Identical stories of arrest and abuse went on and on, just with different names and places. Only the torture was uniform. Thousands more were just referred to as 'unnamed.' None of them looked the slightest bit revolutionary. They just disappeared, like Marcela and Paulo. The Argentine and Uruguayan press were muzzled and most Americans were completely unaware that a campaign of civilian torture and murder was going on. Willie was shocked to read that a third of the disappeared were women. Some were abducted with their small children and others were pregnant, or became so while in detention, usually through rape by guards and torturers. Pregnant prisoners were routinely kept alive until they'd given birth. "Our bodies were a source of special fascination," one of the detainees emotionally reported to Amnesty International. "They said my swollen nipples invited the 'prod' — the electric cattle prod, which was used in torture. They presented a truly sickening combination—the curiosity of little boys, the intense arousal of twisted men." Sixty students from Manuel Belgrano High School in Buenos Aires were 'disappeared' simply for having joined their student council. Victims were abducted as they stepped off buses, as they walked home from work or school, or in midnight raids of private residences.

Cristina and her older sister Marcela were hardly socialists, although they shared private opinions about the deteriorating state of fairness and equality in this abundant land. Her husband Paulo had gotten involved in the trade union movement while in university, although he was neither vocal nor particularly active anymore. Alma's nephew, Ricardo showed Willie a different, apolitical, and less sober side of the family. Alma told Willie, "You're living proof that Americans don't know the first thing about their neighbors. You should go back and see the rest of the continent. Buy a motorcycle, like Che. Take buses and trains. Look around and see how people live and write it all down. The press is silent there. Everyone is scared. You will write a great story." She shook her head and pointed her index finger towards her temple. Alma teased Willie about being the 'next Che' after his return and professed desire to go back later in the year. His parents were tolerant of his past trip, positioned as a 'short post college break', but he hadn't figured out how to broach a longer return trip that he couldn't afford.

Willie went back to bartending at the Irish pub in Old Town. The evening schedule and money were decent, although he had to suffer the indignity of living at home to save money so he could go back to Buenos Aires in the fall. He never considered writing or journalism as a career, but Willie knew he needed to take a notebook this time and keep a record. There wasn't much in his past that suggested an aptitude for travel or telling stories. He was never kept a diary, nor had he gone much of anywhere as a child. He'd only roared around Europe on trains after high school with several privileged friends for three weeks, learning very little, except that European beer is strong. Still Alma's advice was encouraging and it felt like 'a calling.' She was the first person to suggest that Willie Thomas might have something to say worth listening to. No one at O'Shaughnessy's Pub was interested in South America.

Willie knew his parents would laugh at another request for a loan to go back to South America. He could frame it as an advance toward his new career as a journalist, had that been something he'd considered – and mentioned – before. Several times he raised the subject of Orlando Letelier's death and connection to Chilean secret police and death squads. His parents were puzzled why their son, who had shown no interest in much of anything, would glom onto – and try to solve -- an international terrorist murder. "Isn't this something the FBI is investigating?" his father commented. "What do you know that they don't? Hell, you barely speak Spanish."

Big Bill made his mind up that his son's 'aimlessness' was a correctable condition. *The boy had three months to sew his oats and now he is back ... bartending with a college degree? Spending his nights in a bar rather than days in an office? The boy mopes around the house, interrupting poor Alma and then goes to the neighborhood pub to work. That's quite a post-college existence. It's time for him to grow up!* No one ever had to tell Big Bill to grow up or to get a job. One moment he was a patriotic kid volunteering for his country; a year later he was back at the University of Virginia on the G.I. Bill. Two years later, he started a career as an assistant loan officer for Riggs Bank. Twenty-five years later, he was a senior vice president.

Willie enjoyed his back and forth correspondence with Cristina. She was spunky and serious – Alma was right about that. He liked her fearlessness and sense for justice. She was willing to risk her life for her sister and that was as heroic as anything Willie had ever seen. They exchanged letters and cards every few weeks. If he was going to return, he needed to fully understand the risks of getting involved with this family. That had been Alma's advice from the start about returning to South America. She never discouraged Willie and did believe that a good book, or better an in-depth expose on the sins of the government, would help bring the world's attention to her homeland. Alma just didn't want to involve him in a dangerous situation.

In her first response, Cristina wrote back sharply, welcoming his return to the 'gates of Hell' and laying out her conditions for Willie traveling to search for her sister. She planned to take leave from the architectural firm on September 1st and she attached several news clippings about the deteriorating state of affairs from the *Buenos Aires Herald*. Her handwriting, grasp of English slang and tonality surprised him. *You need to fully understand this stuff if you really want to do this. Particularly if you get involved with my family's dirty laundry.* Was he up to this? Willie wasn't sure, but it beat listening to drunks, night after night, complaining about their jobs or their ex-wives, or the hapless Washington Deadskins. Then there was his father.

Cristina and Alma made Willie feel alive with something important to do … or with something to prove. His life so far required little risk, and no action. The anniversary of his one-year college graduation passed without comment, although Willie felt the raised eyebrows and awkward silences around their home on South Fairfax Street. Only Alma talked to him about something else. "William, if you go, and I hope you do, be careful. I suggested that you go back and write about it. But don't tell anyone while you are there. Foreigners asking questions are not welcome. First world population, third world politics." Alma paused, watching Willie's face droop. "I spoke to my brother Jose-Maria last night and he had a good suggestion. You and Cristina need to have a business cover for your trip; the reason you are in Argentina. Searching for my niece Marcela is not the right answer. Nor is gaining approval to write an expose on the sins of the military junta."

Willie smiled at Alma's candor and energy. She was always thinking about risks and rewards. It was a dangerous place when she left a decade ago. It was far worse now. Militants used to be arrested, but now it was arbitrary depending on where you lived and who your friends were. The only guidance she could give was to stay alert, keep your voice down and be cautious. "Jose-Maria suggested that you and Cristina get some business cards printed up that say you are travel guidebook writers, or something that makes sense for two people traveling around the country, taking notes, asking questions about hotels and sights. It's something to hand a policeman if you are stopped. The police are document crazy and they can throw you in jail if you look at them wrong. They did it to a friend's son."

Willie liked the idea -- *el periodista* would certainly not be the right occupation to put on his arrival card. But 'travel guide researcher' sounded more innocuous … and accurate. He and Cristina were entering a different place with different rules. Cristina had another suggestion. "There's an Australian couple who has written a guide called, 'Across Asia on the Cheap.' Do you think they might be interested in publishing one on South America? Most of the guides I've seen are for rich, older people. We should write them. What's to lose? They might offer us a freelance job. Getting paid would be a good thing."

"Why not?" he answered. "The name fits perfectly with the story. Who knows where this whole trip goes? Traveling around South America and finding your sister isn't a bad goal."

"Travel guide writers we will be, then,' she laughed, happy about her upcoming temporary non-paying occupation.

One early evening, a well-dressed guy came into O'Shaunessy's and sat at the end of the bar. The weary executive looked out of place with his charcoal grey chalk-stripe suit. Willie assumed he was looking for the French bistro on the next block. "Good evening," Willie began, placing the plastic-encased menu on the bar. "There's a Shepherd's Pie special and tonight's drink special is a Pisco Sour. It's like a margarita, but made with a brandy. Sort of a Chilean whiskey sour. Try it, it's refreshing."

The man smiled and put his worn satchel on the empty barstool next to him. "No food tonight, thank you," he answered, putting the menu down. "But a little of your Pinochet Punch sounds delicious," he cracked. "Chile's a beautiful place."

Willie's face lit up. "I'm hopefully headed down later in the year. I'm planning to write a guide book for budget travelers. But first, I need to look around. I've only been in Argentina and Montevideo."

The businessman looked up. "They're going through a tough time. It's either Che … or Pinochet. No in-betweens. You remember that guy who was killed last year in the car bombing?"

"Of course, Carlos Letelier," Willie answered quickly, trying to sound halfway fluent in his pronunciation of the surname -- leh-tehl-YEHR. "Murdered with an American woman last September. They still haven't found the killers. Everyone assumes it's DINA, who hired Cubans to do it." He exhaled, proud to have gotten the names and order right, and hoping his pronunciation didn't completely betray his lack of knowledge. Willie had become sensitive that he was a phony.

The businessman loosened his tie and unfastened his top button, nodding enthusiastically, "Wow, I'm impressed. That's exactly what I hear too. And I work in the State Department. By the way, I'm Ned."

"Willie," he replied, offering his hand. "I've been following this story for the last several months. I was going to a job interview in the District the day the bomb went off. Why isn't the case solved by now? Seems pretty straightforward."

"Well," Ned began, "That's a good question. Several of us have asked it. The sad answer is the United States has few good allies in a tricky region. No one wants to see our major supplier of copper go socialist. I hear the operation just got out of hand. They crossed the line with Letelier and some others in Europe. I'm glad we have a new administration, with new rules of engagement."

"That's a good thing, isn't it?"

"Of course," Ned answered. "Still, Pinochet rules with an iron fist. It's a strange place these days. It'll take some time for this to get sorted out. Until then, it's the wild west. And they happily string up outlaws, as they define them."

"What do you do?" Willie asked. He was excited to be having a real conversation on a subject no one he knew, knew or cared the first thing about. He heard the wild west comparison made before, usually as part of Butch and the Sundance Kid lore.

"I work with USAID. Most of it's in Central America now, but I spent time in Argentina a few years back." Ned shook his head and sipped his drink. "It's a mess," he smiled. "So, you're writing a guide book? What a great idea! They need one. Outside the big cities, South America's empty, particularly in the south. Beautiful lakes, glaciers, mountains all there for the taking. Lovely people too, except for the rulers," he laughed.

Willie leaned in excitedly. It was as though a fairy prince was rescuing him from Washington sports talk. Ned continued. "You should read this great new book on Patagonia by an Englishman named Bruce Chatwin. He was a frustrated art cataloguer at a London auction house and took off to try his luck as a travel writer. It's broken into little chapters that talk about history, funny anecdotes, descriptions of the land and people. It's great. They call it *el fin del mundo*, 'the end of the earth.' It really is. I made it to Ushuaia once. It snows all summer long."

Willie smiled. "I'm not sure where I'm going, other than BA. My partner is an architect who lives there and is setting up the itinerary. She mentioned Cordoba and Mendoza in the west. We're headed into Chile too, I think."

"That's what your sister mentioned," Ned added, abruptly. "I should have mentioned that at the start. We're friends. She asked me to drop by and say hi."

Willie looked up, surprised. "You know Beryl?" All of a sudden, Willie got a knot in his stomach. *What's this?*

"Yeah, we've done a lot of work with her over the past few years," Ned answered, sipping his drink. "She helped us with financing for several of our projects. Rebuilding Managua is expensive," he smiled pausing. "Beryl mentioned you're headed south to seek fame and fortune and that I should stop by."

"Did she mention anything about the other reason I'm going?" Willie's mind was still spinning.

"Yep, you're looking for the missing niece of your housekeeper. Disappeared with her husband last summer. But you haven't told your parents? Right? You and your sister's secret?"

Willie nodded three times. Willie and Beryl talked this through when she was home last month. She promised to do what she could to help locate Marcela and Paulo, although she wasn't optimistic. Beryl heard that less than

10% of people that went in, came out. She knew many people across the region who seemed to know what was going on. She'd make sure Willie had their names, just in case. Argentina was a big country and it looked like they were traveling all over. Willie tried to keep up with the Letelier case in *The Post*, but little seemed to go on. Occasionally an article would appear suggesting progress in the investigation. Then weeks would pass without a peep. No one doubted that the Cubans did it for Pinochet, but the story slowly waned, then withered. The Cubans had moved on to other terrorist projects and were happy to wait the government out.

Ned grinned broadly, reached into his suit pocket and pulled out a pen and began writing on a napkin. "Before I forget. If you get to Mendoza, call this guy." Willie could barely make out the blotted name. LUIS GAJATE 54-261-428-1472. "He's one of the good guys, knows his way around, another Hoya, sorry. He grew up in Bethesda and has been in Mendoza for a year or so. He knows the territory like the back of his hand. He'll be able to help with your guide book. And, do read Chatwin's book. It's a different kind of travel guide. Might give you some ideas for your own book."

Willie looked at the napkin and confirmed the numbers. "This is great. Thanks so much. What do you know of 'los desaparecidos?'" He slowly enunciated *los-des-a-pa-re-ci-dos*. "I've read a few articles. It seems pretty bad. I noticed some women in the Plaza de Armes protesting back in the spring."

Ned grimaced. "It's getting worse. These generals do whatever in the hell they want. The situation is a mess, but who are we to lecture others? Particularly after Watergate and Kent State." He took a sip of his drink. "We raise it when we can. Tossing kids out of helicopters into the Rio Plata is well-known and carried out on a regular schedule. Wednesday afternoons. German efficiency, Latin judgement. Whew!" He drained the remainder of the Pisco Sour and wiped the foam from his lip. "These generals rule by fear. Sadly, it's not our country to tell them what to do. I hear the abductions have gotten random and aggressive." He smiled grimly, as he began to collect his belongings. "But it's as safe as D.C. Just watch yourself and stay away from political rallies. If you get to Mendoza, call Luis." With that, Ned gathered his satchel, put a ten dollar bill on the bar, waved his hand, and disappeared out the door.

Willie watched as the front door closed behind him. Two customers continued bickering about the Redskins and whether Seattle Slew could win the Triple Crown. "Another Pisco?" he asked the pair.

"Nah," one answered. "It was a little sweet for me, but another of Killian's would be great." His fellow barfly nodded and motioned for another Killian's without ever looking at Willie. Willie's moment in an interesting interaction was over. He trudged over to the tap and drew two pints. He had enjoyed the short escape to South America, looking again at the napkin. LUIS GAJATE. Willie shook his head, thinking about his resourceful sister. She always had answers, or knew people who had answers. He suspected her international banking job wasn't as dull as it sounded.

The summer heat labored on and Willie couldn't wait until October, when he planned to head back to Argentina. All he did was work, now up to six nights a week. Interactions with his father, always challenging, had mostly stopped. Willie spent several afternoons on hot days at the Alexandria public library. The library was a free, air-conditioned refuge from the outdoors where he wouldn't know a soul. Willie retrieved microfiche files of old Amnesty International reports and spent days reading, taking notes and making mimeograph copies. There was a big Xerox machine up near the front desk and copies were five cents apiece. Willie was a lazy reader as a youth, but with new-found motivation, he began to devour books and magazines that furthered his understanding of the region. He needed all the background he could fit into his head if he was going to write something about this upcoming journey. He was stuck living at home, working in an Irish pub with lonely and bored patrons who neither knew, nor cared about South America.

Willie took Ned's advice and bought 'On Patagonia.' Chatwin's description of arriving in Buenos Aires on the fifth page hooked him. *"The city kept reminding me of Russia, the cars of the secret police bristling with aerials; women with splayed haunches licking ice-cream in dusty parks; the same bullying statues; the pie-crust architecture, the same avenues that were not quite straight, giving the illusion of endless space and leading out into nowhere."* He remembered those statues and meandering promenades six months ago, although they didn't seem threatening at the time. Maybe he could write a different kind of travel book? He was about to see if Chatwin's comment that 'travel doesn't merely broaden the mind, it makes the mind' was true.

Six

Floresta, Argentina

May – September, 1977

Marcela Caesares lay on her tiny dirty cot, daydreaming. The cement room on the third floor was cold. By late afternoon, the room would warm up a little, better than when she was brought here. Those first summer months nearly a year ago were unbearable. The worst part were the sudden shrieks she could hear through the walls and the loud taunting of more torture to come. The slow, heavy trudge of the step sounds and out-of-breath huffing up the stairs was the lead-in note that *el ejecutor* was coming. And there was absolutely nothing she could do, or say, to make that go away.

Marcela knew from the sounds of passing cars, children giggling, and the occasional horns of commuter trains that she was near a city. She and her husband Paulo were taken in the night and brought here blindfolded. She had not seen him in many months. Marcela was pregnant when she arrived, but had miscarried. The *picana* did what it was supposed to, but she had nothing to tell them. Marcela was an artist, not a revolutionary. Her husband, Paulo cared more about that stuff than she did, but he just encouraged workers to support trade unions. It was the only way he saw to affect change without violence. How and why she was here were questions Marcela had long ago given up trying to answer. One day, she and Paulo were newlyweds. The next day, their lives were shattered and a man she couldn't see was putting an electric cattle prod into her vagina. She told them everything she knew. *Yes, my father had known a few of the Tupamaros in Pando. No, he wasn't a member or a sympathizer, just a neighbor. We raised cattle. And yes, my husband supported labor unions. What is the crime in that?* Being covered in human excrement didn't change her answers. They let up on her after a few months, so now Marcela lay on her bed and daydreamed about a different life. It was simply about keeping herself sane, although some days early on, she wished they had turned up the juice of the *picana* to end the pain. Marcela knew her fate rested with these animals, so she kept quiet, took her torture, and tried not to think about her lost baby and missing husband. As hard as it was, she knew she needed to maintain her composure and develop a plan to get out of here. They had stolen her motherhood and sexuality, but not her hope.

Marcela was still adjusting to the rhythms of monotony and fear. The first few months were a nightmare, literally. Marcela was brought down three floors to the basement at all hours, where she was repeatedly questioned, and having no answers about associates, safe houses and trade union organizers, she was tortured. She got used to the *picana*, but never to waterboarding. Pain was tolerable; not being able to breathe with a torrent of water being poured over her nose and mouth terrified her. They kept asking Marcela

"¿quiénes son sus asociados?" She always answered honestly, "Solo soy un artista." It went along like that for three months. Some days, Marcela would be spared, particularly if the burns or welts from prior beatings were inflamed. She was four-months pregnant when she arrived; they were newlyweds looking forward to family life together when they were kidnapped. She miscarried a month later, after sustained beatings and shock treatments.

The mouthiest guard was named Rafael Sánchez, who called himself *el ejecutor*. He was in his late twenties and appeared to be the only one who enjoyed his job. Marcela never saw his face. He had a gruff country accent with a lisp and a fat stomach, a small prick and limited stamina. He wore a big belt, like a rodeo champion, that he made her carefully unbuckle, as he talked dirty. Sánchez enjoyed the twice-weekly ritual and he always provided a small towel for her to clean him up after his ejaculation.

The youngest guard named Enrico was in his early twenties, but he didn't participate. He was shy and seemed repelled by the goings on. As a result, he did a lot of the janitorial work, mostly moving a bucket and mop around all day. Enrico was a handsome boy from the south; blond, tall, with rosy cheeks. He talked about wanting to go to Detroit to work on an assembly line. A friend told him the UAW paid eleven dollars an hour. None of the guards understood that unions were for working people. There was a lot of information flying around, most of it untrue.

Marcela suspected the warden, Jaime, had a crush on her. He was a proud, patriotic man in his mid-thirties, who was happy to re-educate this artist that socialism was ruining their great country. He liked arguing with her, citing all kinds of statistics about the deaths the leftists had caused and how Argentina was going to the dogs before National Reorganization. *"Remember inflation before National Reorganization? It was 5000% per year. Now it's only 300% a year."*

"No, Argentina isn't about to be overrun by socialists," she assured him on separate occasions. "Did you know that a helicopter loaded up with fifteen or twenty kids takes off every Wednesday afternoon and drops their payload in the Rio Plata?" Jaime hadn't heard about this.

Herman stayed in the kitchen and did most of the cooking. He was quiet and older, probably a lifelong military man. He was reed thin with a pronounced stoop, a bent stick pin of khaki, brought on by years of government-issued bedding. Herman's voice was sad and modest, but he loved talking about football. "This new kid, Maradona, who plays for the Juniors is just sixteen and will be the best in the world. Mark my word." Marcela wasn't a huge football fan, but Herman was gentle and conversation about Argentina's chances in next year's World Cup passed the time.

Marcela pitied them. They were stuck here torturing people or housing them until they could be executed. She felt nothing toward her captors besides pity, except of course for *el ejecutor* who she dreamed of slowly torturing. It had been two months since the last *picana* treatment. She always knew it was him, because he had to pause on the landings to catch his breath, before he continued his slow assault on the stairs. He enjoyed taunting all the prisoners, threatening them with torture on the days he wasn't torturing them.

Part of Marcela's daily ritual was to determine where she was. It was a big building, with at least four floors. She counted the steps when being taken between floors. The tooting of car horns and whooshing of passing traffic meant she was in a city, she assumed a Buenos Aires suburb. Torture took place on the second floor and she was housed one floor above. She knew that for sure, never getting used to the screams coming up through the concrete stairwell that operated as a daily echo chamber. The prisoners ate on the first floor, where there were offices and other rooms. The rooms for the guards must be on the fourth floor, as she never climbed stairs above where her cell was. There was a basement but it wasn't used for much, besides storage.

Life, such as it was, improved a few months ago. Marcela laughed at the whole notion of being gratified for not being tortured. It was all about getting through each day without losing her mind. There were times she thought her head might explode in grief. Early on after Paulo and the baby disappeared, she wanted to kill herself and hoped they would do it for her. It was the sameness, the boredom, the time all alone that ate at her. The slow process of losing hope.

Marcela calculated she'd been imprisoned in this building for nine months. The first few months were a horrible hallucination as the days lost shape and outside events didn't occur. Marcela mostly remembered how hot and stinky it was. There were only a few fans on the first floor and throbbing heat lingered in the concrete walls well past dark. The smells of daily sins hung throughout the stuffy structure. She occasionally overheard the radio in the kitchen – that old man really liked football. The enthusiasm of the announcers reminded Marcela of a world outside going on without her and the World Cup was coming next year. After three months, Jaime halted her torture. "This artist woman has nothing to say, leave her alone. She's no socialist."

What also recently changed was that Jaime had enlisted Marcela to create counterfeit passports. It wasn't a profession she much admired, but Marcela enjoyed the intricacy and steps that had a beginning-middle-end process, with a useful piece of art at the completion. False travel documentation was a necessity for a system intent on changing – and erasing – people's identities. Military officers often required different identities to infiltrate neighboring countries to kidnap activists who fled Argentina. Jaime noticed her neat penmanship and doodles on the wall of her cell. "Do you draw pictures?" he asked one day.

"Yes, I used to. I made prints, you know, big posters. I made T-shirts too."

"Of Che?"

Marcela snickered. "No, but wish I did. Young people admire Che. Particularly his beret. He's a brand now."

Jaime didn't understand her comment. Brands are things people consume or burn on cattle. "He was a revolutionary, a communist."

"Like me?"

Jaime could tell that Marcela was making fun of him. "No, I believe you are a capitalist at heart," he replied. "You were raised with money. Probably on some estancia. I can tell by your attitude."

"I'm flattered," Marcela deadpanned, "but you are wrong. We had some land, but never any money. We were cattle farmers."

"I don't understand why some people fight against their own interests," Jaime continued. "Why do you want to make less money and pay more taxes?"

"Because that's what a fair society does. The well-being of the people is more important than the individual. Otherwise we are back to feudalism."

Jaime had heard this palaver before. Equality and fairness are great, but who is doing all the work? And why should I work harder, just so I can give it to someone else not willing to work as hard as me? "I have a business proposition for you," he smiled. "That is if you believe in hard work and free markets? I would like assistance in the production of documents. Principally passports, but there are other printed materials that the government needs help with. With the improved economic performance since national reorganization, there is tremendous demand for travel. Surely better than with socialists running things?" He looked over to see if his sales pitch was working. It didn't appear to be. "Look at Cuba! Argentines are wealthier and want to see the world. And this will allow you to work alone in the basement. No more funny business."

Aside from breaking the law, Marcela could only laugh at the irony of being a lifelong, law-biding citizen who is sent to prison so that she can become a crook. She enjoyed the craftsmanship of the print making process, from the design to the transfer of the waxen image to the limestone, the etching, the addition of oils and inks applied to the pages in the passport. It passed the time steadily and easily. Marcela knew the real use of these falsified passports. She hated supporting the regime, but quickly realized that this skill could, at some point, be put to better use. This was no time for principled morality and a return to the *picana*. It was time to figure out how to get herself out of here. And probably Jaime too, although he didn't know it yet. She had all the time in the world to figure out how.

Rafael Sánchez was irritated that his special privileges were taken away. First, the warden stopped him from interrogating the artist woman and forbade him from disciplining her. Then he set her up in the basement to make passports. Sánchez acknowledged that her work supported the government – a good and necessary activity, but the warden gave her a lot of perks and freedom. She got to spend all day alone in a cool basement, and he wasn't allowed to touch her. That made him madder.

He marched down to the basement one afternoon. "What do you know of the two women who were just brought in? The records say they are Uruguayan."

Marcela turned to him. "Sorry, there are 2.8 million Uruguayans. Afraid I don't know them." She turned her attention back to her engraving, enjoying the power to safely ignore *el ejecutor.*

"I bet these new girls are better than you." Sánchez smiled with a crude gesture.

"No doubt they are better at it than you are," she answered without looking at him. Sánchez wasn't completely sure what to make of that smart ass exchange, but the two new girls were scared and willing and that's all that mattered.

"How much is the boss paying you to make these passports?"

"Nothing. I'm slave labor, after all. You should know that. These are for the Argentine government. I suspect they will be given to the military so they can kidnap more innocent young people and give you something to do."

Her remarks had become increasingly disrespectful. The artist woman sometimes talked in riddles, typical sassy rich kid. It's always easy to be a critic. Sánchez could swear that he'd seen Spanish and Brazilian passports, and she certainly was busy. As the ranking number two officer at the facility, he deserved to be cut in to whatever commerce was going on. He needed to discuss all of this with the warden.

"I've noticed the artist prisoner has freedoms that the others don't. I believe this will lead to a loss of discipline throughout this unit," he mentioned to the warden the next morning.

"She is fulfilling an order from my superiors. It is of no concern to you." Jaime had grown tired of Sánchez, and knew he could cause trouble. He was a stupid blabbermouth who went too far with everything. And the stuff he'd done to the female prisoners was a crime. Sánchez also needed to get some exercise and stop eating empanadas, noticing his bursting pair of khaki pants held up with a stitched truca belt. What a pig!

"I noticed she was making Spanish passports, too."

"What of it?"

"Why does the Army need Spanish passports?"

"Don't ask me. I just take orders from the government. Who they give these to is of no concern to me. I suggest you mind your own business, unless you want me to raise your concern directly with the commander. There are things going on out of our control." Jaime was tired of all his nosy behavior. Things were moving along fine now. No one needed to involve this asshole.

Rafael Sánchez could tell something was off. The warden had been vague – *I just take orders from the government? Is that so?* Increasingly, Sánchez noticed the warden leaving the building a few days a week with two-three large parcels and returning several hours later. And the girl in the basement was always working ... or sleeping. She was even allowed to take her meals there and once in a while

Herman would bring a small plate of empanadas down to her.

Marcela got used to the rhythms of her day at her little table in the basement and was mostly left alone. The work was tedious, but the time passed quickly. Marcela enjoyed the precision of taking a black and white photograph and building a story with a place and date of birth, a full name and their travels, with the addition of visas and stamps. She could produce up to four passports a day if she wasn't interrupted. There was nothing more satisfying than days and nights passing by quickly.

Jaime was thirty-seven and single. He joined the military half his life ago after secondary school with visions of seeing the world. His older brother had risen quickly to a captain's rank in the navy and he was now stationed at Port Belgrano in the far south of the country. Jaime looked forward to being posted somewhere important one day, and he was frustrated at the progression of his career. He accepted the government view that socialists were taking over the country, but he hadn't been curious enough to understand what was really going on. Jaime supported the inquisitions up to a point, but increasingly he questioned the government's torture tactics. Why were they still doing it to all these innocent kids? It made no sense to him. Many of these prisoners still belonged in secondary school. There were true revolutionaries who needed to be captured and punished.

"You see what the socialists do every day?" Jaime continued. He gave up trying to convince Marcela of anything, but he enjoyed the banter. It helped pass the time. "They kill innocent people. Good people trying to make this country successful. Why do they kidnap the head of Ford? An American company employing lots of Argentines to make cars for us to drive around? It's self-defeating."

"What? Like a Fairlane?" Marcela fired back. She remembered the car and two chunky officers who barged into their apartment and took them away. It was a Ford, she remembered the script in the oval logo fastened to the grill of the ugly car. Jaime didn't appear to understand the reference and that was okay. There was only so much to teach him on any given day.

"I agree about kidnappings and murders. But, there is a balance. You put me in jail for nothing. I'm an artist. What did I do? Do you really think people like me want to overthrow the government? Look at me."

Jaime had listened to Marcela for months now. She was talkative and opinionated when she got going. He liked that she wasn't fearful and spoke her mind. Still, he thought, people like her pretend to be patriots, always talking about what is wrong with the country and how to fix it. They are always complaining about their rights. "Blah, blah, blah. Do we really want to end up like Cuba? Hot, poor, and sloppily-dressed?"

"Jaime, we are similar. Proud citizens who want to make Argentina great again." She paused, judging how much he decided to listen to. "I just think the government doesn't value us. Look, they put you, a patriotic soldier, here to look after me, a young innocent woman, an artist. What a waste of a good and talented soldier!"

Jaime had to agree with that comment, although he thought he remembered that she was Uruguayan. No matter. *What was a talented soldier doing here?* This surely wasn't the career track that his brother was slotted in. He inquired about promotions several times, and they assured him the country valued his service, but needed him to fight the internal revolutionaries. "There's no greater enemy now than these socialists from within." That was always the answer. Jaime didn't see the threat in the same way. Sure, there were bad people who deserved torture for sedition, but there were many innocent college kids, too. Most of them had never been in a fistfight. He saw what the police brought in and wondered if all of these children belonged here. Increasingly, there was less and less paperwork around the prisoners. *Just keep them here and try to get them to talk. We'll follow up with the record keeping next week.*

Jaime had been stuck in this outpost for nearly three years now. His reporting staff consisted of four people, including a cook. It wasn't exactly the command of a battleship. Marcela guessed there were 8-10 people being held, although she never heard them anymore. She thought about Paulo every day, but knew he wasn't here and her baby wasn't here, either. Marcela had a plan to get out of here. But first, she had to make Jaime his own special passport, and most importantly, get him to use it. After that, it would be easy.

The early spring weather didn't lift her spirits. Marcela guessed it was September – over a year of her life wasted.

For what? She continued conversations with Jaime about his future and slowly, she convinced him that he needed another job. Promotions and praise for his critical role in support of the National Reorganization Plan had yet to materialize. A few of the prisoners brought in were clearly revolutionaries and they were duly punished, or sent away. But more and more, the people they brought in were kids. He didn't deserve to waste his talents on babysitting. The artist girl was right – this country's people were better than their leadership. He too needed a new start.

"I've heard that military officers in Venezuela make a very good living," she had mentioned to Jaime a few times. "The weather is warm and the beaches are beautiful. You should go there on holiday. I suspect the women would fall all over you."

"I guess with all that oil, everyone lives well. I've heard the women are beautiful," Jaime jumped in. "I hear trade winds from the Caribbean Sea blow all the time."

"You are right. Did you know the Miss Universe contest is held there?" Marcela replied. "White sand, clear warm water and no revolutionaries. Soldiers need their R and R so that they are sharp when their country calls on them."

Jaime had to agree with this young woman, although rarely was she this solicitous. "It's hard to get leave. I was planning to meet my brother and his wife for holiday in Bahia Blanca. But my superiors won't allow leave at this time."

"That's too bad. When will they allow you a break?"

"I do not know," he answered plaintively. "Perhaps later in the year?"

Four months ago, Jaime was incorruptible. But then he enlisted Marcela make different kinds of passports that weren't for the military. He was very sly about it, coming down to the basement office with very specific instructions. "Some of my superiors requested that we create these particular passports for citizens desiring to travel abroad." He handed her a list of eight names, photographs and their vital information. "Some of them require identification and places of citizenship." Marcela looked over the list. There were three who needed U.S. passports, one from Venezuela, and another from Colombia.

"I've never made any of these," she answered.

"Those are our orders," Jaime answered sternly. "I have several upstairs in my office that you can examine. These documents are very important and they must be done with the upmost care and quality."

Marcela said nothing, but simply nodded. Jaime was incurious, but he increasingly displayed an entrepreneurial, criminal faculty. He'd picked up some new clients and needed more of her help. She quickly realized that not only was Jaime producing passports for the Argentine military, but he had developed a side business producing counterfeit documents for the general public. Marcela wasn't sure about the timing, but knew this was her ticket out. A brand new life with a new identity. She could easily reinvent herself in an afternoon, but she needed Jaime if this was going to succeed. She wouldn't make it fifty feet outside this prison without him. Marcela had learned a very valuable lesson over the past several weeks. He was corruptible. She just needed more time to move him along.

"Yes, I understand," she replied. "We are going to need new supplies and inks. These shades of green and yellow are hard to match," she noted, pointing to the passport list Jaime had handed her. "The Spanish ones are easy. I will do some testing on the Venezuelan one as they use a special bonded paper."

Jaime didn't really understand the intricacies of passport production and design, particularly paper and card stock, but he nodded. "Yes, we need to make these documents perfect."

"I'll get to work on these right away," she answered. "I want to do a test on the Venezuelan passport before printing it. I'll use a dummy name."

The relationship between Marcela and Jaime had become co-dependent. Jaime needed Marcela to produce the counterfeit passports for the country. He delivered them to the district commander's office every week with a salute. Through a friend, he heard that lots of Argentines were looking to get out ... and were willing to pay. Thirty-five U.S. dollars apiece was the going rate. The more passports Jaime could deliver, the more money he could make. He needed to cut the artist woman in and help her too. She wasn't any kind of socialist, he'd finally concluded, and she didn't deserve to be here in the first place. By mid-winter, Marcela was working through the night, creating up to fifteen passports a week. They split up the money, two-thirds for Jaime, one-third for her. It was fair. The government paid for supplies.

Marcela began planning her escape five months ago just after Jaime recognized her artistic skills and brought her to the basement. Half of her work was for the Argentine government; the rest was for Jaime. She guessed he cleared $500 a month on top of his meager salary. It was their little secret that no one, particularly *el ejecutor,* needed to know about. *'Just doing it for our superiors'* was all either of them said. Now all she had to do was convince Jaime that he belonged on a warm Caribbean beach among the Miss Universe contestants.

Marcela spent one afternoon and most of the next day creating a new Venezuelan passport. It was a simple engraved design, a gold crest affixed to the red cover. It didn't require all the leaping animals and ornamental leaves that other countries had, which took up hours of time to recreate. She wasn't sure how he would react, but now was the time to find out. She had come to trust Jaime; maybe it was their conspiracy to forge illegal passports? Marcela knew that the only way she was leaving was if he was leaving too. She could die here, or make a move now. This was her shot.

"Jaime, I wanted to show you something. I had some extra time this week and made this for you." She picked up the new Venezuelan passport and handed it to him. He felt the heavy stock of the cover, nodding at its quality.

"It's very nice. You've become very skilled at making these documents. My superiors have been very impressed with the quality of our work."

"Go ahead and open it," she encouraged him. "This is the first one I've made and I wanted to make sure that it meets your standards."

He immediately laughed as he opened the passport to the first page. "Wow, where did you find this picture?" Staring back at Jaime was a snapshot of his face, glued into the bonded passport with a red cover. "And who is this handsome man?"

"I needed to do a test and wanted to show it to you. How does it look?"

Jaime looked through the empty passport pages, smiling contentedly. "Not that I would ever need a Venezuelan passport, but I like how this came out." He nodded. He flipped back to the page with his picture.

"Great," she answered. "You can keep it, if you want. It's only a test sample. But now we know I can make Venezuelan passports if you have any willing customers. Not too bad having a passport from the richest country in South America."

Jaime smiled, taken with the photograph of himself. "Where did you get my photograph? I don't remember you ever taking my picture."

"I wanted to surprise you," she answered. "There was a picture of you with some other officers in uniform that I noticed in the kitchen area. I borrowed to make the passport photo. I hope you didn't mind. I put the picture back in the frame."

Jaime looked again at the first page. This desk job had caused him to put on some weight. "No, no," he answered. "This picture makes me look younger ... and fitter. I like this. I'm glad you took this step to test out other passport designs. It will expand our business. Great work."

Marcela was glad to hear his openness. Increasingly, she threw out temptations of a new life as a thirty-seven-year-old businessman from Maracaibo, Venezuela. Within the next few months, with any luck, Jaime Rodriguez will become Sebastian Martinez. He will carry all of the required documentation, including a Banesco checking account. Marcela Caesares, in turn, will become Marcela Rezende, a twenty-nine-year-old reclusive Brazilian artist and photographer, living in Foz do Iguaçu, a frontier town on the border with Argentina and Paraguay. Two perfect places for new starts. She had some time to bring Jaime along, but her first step toward freedom had been received positively.

Seven

Alexandria, Virginia and Buenos Aires, Argentina

September, 1977

"I don't know mamacita, he said he was arriving a week from Friday." Cristina Alvarez's phone call with her Aunt Alma carried an excited air. She had taken leave from her architectural firm until the end of the year. If it took longer, so be it. As with any trip into the unknown, Cristina was excited and had been running around calling people who might help. Usually it was a friend of a friend of a friend and all of it was completely unpredictable. They would arrive in each new place and see what happens. There were several girls who had agreed to talk to her.

Cristina and Willie traded aerograms, a few mailed packages and eight expensive phone calls over the past five months. The itinerary was coming together. Willie was excited and he'd done a lot of research on Argentina and Uruguay since he'd been home. When she met Willie nine months ago, he seemed sweet and well-meaning, but unfocused. He looked like a well-bred, eager-to-please puppy dog. BA and Montevideo were nice urban escapes, but now they would be trudging around provincial cities on a dual mission, looking for her sister and trying to write a travel guidebook.

How they were going to locate and spring her sister and brother-in-law from an unknown prison was the question that neither of them could answer. Cristina's mother was anxious, yet optimistic, still believing that Americans always come to the rescue. In her mind, Willie would arrive with the First Marine Division, tear through the continent, rescue her daughter, and cast out the generals over a long weekend. Everyone agreed that writing a travel guide, or at least using it as a cover to find her older sister, was the best plan. The Australian couple who started *Lonely Planet* guides a few years ago wrote Cristina back that a South American guidebook was a future plan. *We won't be able to reimburse you for your expenses at this point, but would certainly include your recommendations and travel information when we take that project on next year. We will happily accredit your contributions. It's quite a continent with few outsiders. Keep us informed of your travels. Best regards, Tony*

Cristina saw this as a good sign. "They won't pay us, but they were encouraging. And he signed it, it was a personal note. That's good. We are now officially unpaid travel guide writers. Willie, you're in charge of business cards."

"My father will be ecstatic," Willie answered, imagining handing his father this new business card over dinner. The name alone was sure to drive him into a fit. *"So, you want to be a travel guide writer? What are you going to write about? A Lonely Planet? Who's going to pay you? Your lone customer? When will this phase end? Son, you really are a disappointment."*

"No, I'm serious," she answered. "You need to take this beyond just a travel guide of places to see. Like what Alma suggested to you about writing 'The Willie Diaries'? I've listened to you over the past six months talking about writing something. Well, start writing. Keep a detailed record of the sights and hotels. But also write something more important. About what's going on here. This story must be told."

Willie smiled uncertainly. She was right again, of course. Maybe she should be the one writing the damn story? Cristina Alvarez was extremely competent at everything else she touched.

"C'mon Willie. You have the responsibility to tell the bigger story when you return home. This story is about searching for the disappeared, however it turns out. You've read the Amnesty Reports. No Argentine can write that story and stay. They tossed Bob Cox out of the country – he was the only voice talking about these crimes happening right before our eyes." Cristina continued. "The world needs to know what is going on. Instead we're silent and hope it just goes away. How sad we've become."

Cristina was hesitant at first – all of it seemed so slapdash and risky. The last thing she wanted was to babysit Willie, no matter how noble his intentions. But now their mission had momentum and suddenly it felt urgent. The disappearances had worsened over the past six months and

Cristina concluded that she was wasting her life drawing roofing plans for a new high rise down on the waterfront. She had to do something, anything, right now to find her sister.

Buenos Aires remained a proud city, tiptoeing into soulful protest as Porteños tried to go about their lives as they always had, with their heads high and shoes polished. The mothers at Plaza de Mayo, just a handful back in April, now spilled outside the square and their wailing began to attract broader and more sympathetic audiences. Women in white headscarves holding hand-made signs with pictures and names of their children embroidered on scarves slowly circled the square, like a small defenseless army.

Cristina wrote to friends, relatives, and friends of relatives. She got feedback that leaving her job at the architectural firm to write a guidebook was crazy. She'd never been outside of Argentina and Uruguay, and now she was going to tell others where to go in Surinam and Paraguay? Who in the hell goes there anyway? Neither Cristina nor Willie thought through much other than rescuing her sister. Willie had gotten himself excited that he could be the next Bruce Chatwin, if only he could write a story that people wanted to read.

The lure of a travel story, narrated by him, carried Willie through the long, steamy summer beside the Potomac as he poured pints of Killian Red. He regularly corresponded with Cristina, learned more about where he was going, and listened distractedly to Washington sports fans. The Washington Bullets were improving, but the pub's regulars weren't ready for pro basketball yet. The Senators had left for Arlington to become the Texas

Rangers. Professional hockey was a lightly-attended
curiosity and the Capitals were atrocious. He couldn't get
out of town quickly enough.

Buenos Aires, Argentina

"Hola," Willie shouted, exiting customs, as he noticed a
familiar, stylish woman in the arrivals area wearing round
sunglasses with a tortoise shell frame.

"Bienvenido a buenos aires," Cristina replied, waving
her hand. Willie had cleaned himself up, his hair was cut
and combed. "I see you took my advice and look like a
good young Republican," she cracked, giving him an
awkward hug. "You take direction well." She was dressed
casually, in jeans with a cotton blouse. Her hair was longer
and thicker.

Willie was still trying to get the airplane fog lifted, as
they drove towards the city. It was 8:15 in the morning. He
needed coffee, or sleep. He gazed out of the window, as
smoke-belching dented trucks stumbled along the highway,
backfiring and wheezing as they entered the city. Traffic
was heavy, although there was a cool breeze blowing in his
window. It was a pretty morning, as Cristina steered her
Fiat down the exit ramp. "I've continued to read what I
can, but your government does a good job of hiding the
truth. Those Amnesty reports scared the shit out of me."
His eyes looked up to see the seedy Madero docks, as

Cristina turned right onto another street, shaded by taller buildings.

"You'll get used to it, sorry to say," she deadpanned. "My apartment is just up ahead. You've been here, you remember?" she said, pointing to a café up ahead on the right. "You walked me home from dinner that night." Cristina smiled and pulled into a garage underneath a non-descript apartment block. She parked and they unloaded the small Fiat and walked up three flights of stairs to her apartment. She unlocked the door to #3 and entered the small, but clean and cheerful apartment. "As we discussed, your bed is the sofa over there under the window. I'm sorry, it's the best I can do. Architects are underpaid here, just like everywhere."

Willie smiled. Everyone he knew was underpaid, if they weren't unemployed, like him. The apartment was open and cheerful. There was a large blue and white pastel over the mantle that looked like an island in the Mediterranean. "My mother painted it," she volunteered. "She's an artist, Alma's older sister. My mother could never afford the go to Greece. So, she brought it here with her imagination. We Argentines have to be delusional." She snickered. "I'm just waiting for the economic miracle the generals are promising."

Willie fumbled through his duffle bag and pulled out a flat rectangular package. "I figured it might keep you inspired while we're on the road." He handed the wrapped parcel over. "At least, it won't break," Willie added. "He's America's best from what I hear."

Cristina broadly smiled as she slowly pulled back the tape and opened the package, neatly filleting the paper with a knife. She laughed. "My mother taught me to save wrapping paper that I like." She looked at the black and red cover of 'The Natural House' and caught her breath. "Wow! It's Wright's autobiography. It's beautiful. Where did you find this? It hasn't been in print in twenty years." She immediately began thumbing through the book. "This is wonderful. Thank you."

"Well, I have to admit I had a little help. My sister suggested it. I'm not much of an expert on architecture, but I have heard of Frank Lloyd Wright."

"It will be the first book on my empty coffee table over there." Cristina stood up. "I'm headed to the office to sort out several things before we leave tomorrow. Get some rest and walk around the neighborhood this afternoon. We'll have an early dinner, say nine o'clock?" She stood up and began walking to the door. "I left an extra key on the table. San Telmo's fun and very casual. You should go up to the Plaza where the mothers are gathered. It's three times the size it was in March. At least it will make you feel like you are doing something important. I walk by there every day to remind me that I have a purpose. Tomorrow, we go to Cordoba. It's where they met in university and her husband's from there. There is someone we can talk to."

Willie lay on the sofa bed, tossing back and forth, trying to squeeze in a short nap, between the bright shards of sunlight ricocheting through his tired, dry eyelids. He couldn't sleep. Part of it was jet-lag; he could never sleep on planes, but most of it was just excitement. He was impressed with Cristina's organization and attention to detail. She reminded him of his sister. Utterly competent and serious, but always cool about it – three traits he aspired to.

He picked up the Fodor's guide book and turned to the section on Cordoba. A progressive city of two million people, located in the foothills in the center of the country. The Jesuits originally settled Cordoba in the 1600s, but were run out 200 years later. The city center was dominated by a huge complex of churches, cloisters and the National University of Cordoba. There are good hikes outside the city. The guidebook touted the city's 'youthful energy.'

"Cordoba is an old colonial town. It predates BA," Cristina wrote earlier in the summer. "The bus takes all day. I think it's ten hours, train's about the same. There are three places we can stay: the Hotel Lady, which I hear is friendly and has hot showers, the Central near the bus station, or the Hotel Entre Rios. All three suit our budget – rooms are $4 per night." Cristina had neatly written down the names of cheap hotels and restaurants in several cities. "I've also been told that the Romagnolo next to the train station is casual but very good for a meal. My friend told me to try the veal Milanese."

Cristina also collected more important information from friends about Cordoba. There were rumors of a prison outside of town called La Perla. She knew the sister of a woman named Claudia who was held there for nearly a year and was released only after her family raised the $5,000 ransom. "She is one of the lucky ones," Cristina sneered. "She was an arts student like Marcela, who got on the wrong side of things. I might be able to meet with her. She lives in Cordoba with her parents now."

Willie opened his new diary. At this point it was an empty spiralbound lined school notebook that he had crammed into the side pocket of his backpack. He jotted down a line he remembered from Che's *Motorcycle Diaries* right after he bought the book: "I finally felt myself lifted definitively away on the winds of adventure toward worlds I envisaged would be stranger than they were, into situations I imagined would be much more normal than they turned out to be." He hoped to be inspired and to find something he was good at. It was nearing eleven and sleep was hopeless. He could hear the distant squealing of truck brakes and aggravated car horns.

Over dinner that night, Cristina talked about the challenges of two young people travelling in the countryside, asking questions of strangers. Better not scare anyone, particularly a provincial policeman, inquiring about a couple who might have come through town a year ago, she was warned. The one snapshot she had of her bohemian pregnant sister and a tall, long-haired man with a moustache would instantly arouse suspicions. "We have to make it work. Otherwise, a Ford Fairlane will be pulling up one night outside our hotel."

"What does that mean?" Willie asked.

"The Ford Fairlane is the unmarked vehicle of choice for the police. Sort of like a sedan-sized hearse. Our family name is listed somewhere deep within their data-base. Record-keeping is one of the regime's few strengths. They've learned it from the old Nazis they're harboring around the country."

Willie laughed nervously. He hadn't thought that government abductions ran in the family. "Plymouth Furies are the popular police cars in the States. Most of the time they are marked. But I'll remember that," Willie replied. "Unmarked police cars always scare me. They get to be cops only when they want to."

"It's bad here. A car just shows up, takes someone from their home, and they are never seen again. The furtive quality scares me most. There's no rhyme or reason. They make a lot of mistakes that they go to great lengths to cover up. 'Oops we got the wrong person! 'Oh well, too late now.' *Boom, boom.* " She paused, trying to slow down and catch her breath. "I'll wake you at six. The train leaves at seven."

Eight

Cordoba, and Mendoza, Argentina

October-December, 1977

They boarded the early train at Retiro station for the daylong trip northwest via Rosario. Cristina had recommended buses, as they were cheaper and usually more prompt. Still, train seats were wide and comfortable and Willie enjoyed the feeling of speed and smoothness, watching the static world rush by as the train picked up speed leaving the station. Willie tried to close his eyes, but he was excited and restless. Cristina sat next to him doodling on a pad that she kept in an oversized satchel.

"You're a leftie?" Willie pointed out, not comfortable with silence. "My sister Beryl is a lefty. You're both smart, creative types. I read somewhere that only ten percent of the world is left-handed. But Einstein and Mozart and a bunch of others were. We call those 'fun facts' in English."

"Don't forget Leonardo da Vinci, Michelangelo, and Pele too," Cristina added. "I think I read the same article. We're a well-represented minority. It must be due to the childhood trauma of being forced to use our right hands. I read that in another article not too long ago. Remember 'sinister' comes from the Latin, *sinesta* for 'left'? It's a conspiracy against us that goes back centuries," she chuckled.

"What are you working on?" Willie noticed a whimsical drawing of what looked to be the front of city building. Cristina had drawn oversized columns and a gabled roof with an arch framed entrance. It was fun looking, like a stage set out of a Disney movie. From time to time, she took a colored pencil out of a box to accent a detail of the elevation, then carefully put it back in the slot. Willie liked seeing an artist work.

"Oh, nothing. Just a new project we won in La Plata. A children's museum. I'm taking a leave of absence, but the sketching relaxes me. Drawing pictures, like a child."

"You're lucky to have a skill. And a passion."

"I've been drawing pictures of buildings since I was six. My parents worried it was an obsession."

Willie chuckled. "Well, at least they let you write with your left hand. A children's museum sounds fun. Most museums are big and cold looking. Is that a particular style?" The line drawing of the entry elevation with oversized columns and pediments was precise, with bright-

colored pencil accents and fanciful signage. Another row of
columns looked like kids doing handstands.

"They call it Post-Modern. Don't ask me why?
Architects enjoy having important-sounding names for
styles. There was one in the 1950s called Neo-Brutalism.
Very self-important, but uncomfortable-sounding."

The terms whizzed by Willie's ear. He was glad the
Frank Lloyd Wright book was a hit and he noticed it alone
on the table as they locked up the apartment. Cristina had
given instructions about forwarding mail to her neighbor
who lived upstairs. Hearing words like 'post-modern' and
'neo-brutal' for the first time made him feel stupid, but he
was glad that his gift was well-received. "Want anything
from the dining car?"

"A coffee would be great."

Willie stood and walked unsteadily back to the dining
car as the train wobbled along the track. The suburbs had
thinned, leaving an increasingly open expanse out the train
window. Cristina possessed the same focus and self-
confidence as his sister. *Maybe something will rub off on me?*
Willie thought about her color-pencil sketches and printing
style. *Did she come by that naturally? Or did they teach you to print
in architecture school?* Suddenly he felt like a fraud. He went to
college for five years and came out with no skills. Why am I
here again?

That unanswered question made him irritable and
lonely. He was tired from the flight down and his back
hurt. "Dos cafés con leche y azucar. Gracias." The

attendant nodded. Willie felt better with his successful exchange. *The man might even think that Spanish is my native tongue.* "Your welcome, sir," came the reply with a smile as he placed the beverages on the counter.

"What's the matter?" Cristina asked, after Willie delivered the coffee. "You look unsettled."

Willie looked up from his funk. "Sleeping problems."

"You're wondering why you are here? Don't worry, me too."

Willie smiled. Clairvoyance was another skill he lacked. "I'm glad you are here, Willie. It will be good for both of us. A woman can't really travel alone, particularly doing something as irrational as this. But you came into our life and volunteered to help. You don't know my family, and you are doing this for your housekeeper. That is very heroic, but crazy. I know we talked about this before, but thank you. You are very American, my aunt joked about it … in the best possible way."

Willie laughed nervously. No one had ever put his name and heroic in the same sentence. He wasn't sure why he was here, other than he didn't have a clue about what to do with his life. Nothing had grabbed him, yet. "When did you decide to be an architect?"

"Always, since I was a child. It was just one of those things I liked to do growing up. Drawing and playing with blocks. I wasn't much of a girl for dolls, but I liked dollhouses. Architecture is a fun profession. You get to think like a kid again. How should a museum for children be designed? How do we light a fire in a child's imagination? And make it approachable enough for a bunch of wealthy donors too."

Willie laughed nervously at her easy intensity. It was as if she lived in another world. *Lighting a fire in a child's imagination? Who thinks like that? In her second language?*

"You're lucky you have found something you love doing." He was still absorbing her mastery of the English language.

"What do you like to do? What was your major at university?" Cristina was puzzled at the lax American attitude toward college. It seemed to be more of a finishing school geared to connections rather than a place to learn a vocation. In her world, university education was far too expensive to waste on an uncommitted student.

"I don't know. Nothing special. I was an English major, but not a lot of it stuck, I'm afraid. I liked hanging out, going to bars, having fun. I look back now and see that I wasted a lot of time. It takes Americans longer to grow up. English is my mother tongue and I still can't come up with phrases like 'lighting a fire in a child's imagination.'"

Cristina smiled at the compliment. Willie was sweet and sincere, yet didn't seem to have much of his own fire within. But he had taken this risk and maybe it would jumpstart his future? She hoped he would write something important. She encouraged him to put aside an hour a day to jot down his thoughts and observations, perhaps over a glass of wine or beer. She also reminded Willie that writing was a very cheap occupation to pursue. It takes up a lot of time, little space and costs nothing. There was bound to be a lot of downtime on this trip. Cristina carried a list of people who might have known Marcela. She heard about a few girls who were released and might be willing to talk. They might get lucky, but it was also important for Cristina to better understand what her sister was going through.

"We've talked about this several times and I will say it again. You need to write an expose on these disappearances. No one is talking about it. No Argentine can get away with writing about it. Look what they did to *The Herald* editor? Threatened his family and made him leave the country. The generals have gone completely nuts." Cristina paused, exhaling, her expressive left hand clenched. "I'm sorry. This gets me really worked up. How did this country end up here?" She sat back. "I don't care if you decide to be a journalist or a novelist, or a real estate salesman, but you have an obligation to write about this."

Willie nodded, looking back at Cristina sheepishly.

"Well, nothing like the present," she continued. "It's sad that no one in America even knows about what these governments are doing to their people." Cristina always got aggravated when she realized no one in the United States thought about South America. She leaned forward in her seat, turning to Willie. "Your job is to tell the whole story. The good and the bad. We talked about Bruce Chatwin's book, 'On Patagonia." You did read it?"

"Of course," he replied quickly. He liked that there were expectations for him on this trip and that she was relentless in pushing him. He was excited to enter an exotic world and, for the first time he could remember, he had something to accomplish that people were counting on.

The train rambled through the pleasant, rolling landscape toward Cordoba. Willie envied Cristina's ability to get lost in her pursuits. She was able to sit beside him, make small talk, then go into a creative trance of sketching, erasing, and more sketching. She was good at quiet and concentration; he wasn't, at least not yet.

Cristina had spent the last few months talking to close friends and relatives. There was little to go on, but a very brave girl named Claudia agreed to talk to her. There were two detention centers outside Cordoba – La Perla and the Campo la Ribera. Their plan was to check into the Entre Rios, a hotel near the train station, before splitting up. Cristina planned to meet Claudia at a nearby café, while Willie toured the city. He'd gather rail and bus schedules, talk to desk clerks and café owners. He planned to collect brochures from landmark sites and go on a tour of the Jesuit Block and Estancias.

Willie knew little about the Jesuits, or Catholicism for that matter. He was raised Episcopalian, to the extent religion entered his life. He applied to Georgetown and was told that nothing rivalled a Jesuit education, long on learning, faith and service. But Willie's unremarkable college board scores steered his college choices to nearby places, like American University and GW. He tried to engage Cristina on the state of religion in Argentina, but she rolled her eyes. "C'mon, you expect the Catholic church to have a constructive role in this reorganization? It is a long, long story."

At 3:30, Cristina entered the small non-descript café near the train station and sat at a table in the back, next to the kitchen. It was quiet after the lengthy lunch period. She ordered a Fanta. Ten minutes later, a pretty, dark-haired woman entered. She instantly reminded Cristina of her sister, Marcela – the dark bohemian uniform and short pixie haircut. She, too, was long limbed, with the quiet grace of a dancer. She smiled awkwardly and introduced herself as Claudia. She put her small handbag on the chair beside her carefully, looking around the space. They traded a story about their mutual connection, an architect Cristina knew from BA, who was from Cordoba. Cristina showed her a picture of Marcela and Paulo.

She studied it and shook her head. "Never seen them before. I'm sorry." She looked down and took a small bite of empanada and re-examined the picture. "They could have been at Campo la Ribera. We were kept blindfolded most of the time, so I never got much of a look at anyone. I'm sorry you've come all this way."

Claudia passed the pictures back to Cristina. She began to shake and sniffle. "It's hard. There were same pictures that my family showed people. I'm lucky, I guess. But the memories …" she began haltingly, before stopping.

"You're welcome to tell me what you went through. Or not. It's okay. I promise not to write anything down."

Claudia's eyes darted around the café. The waiter was in the kitchen, washing dishes, no threat of a nosy informer in this establishment. She looked around, then began, "As soon as we arrived at the camp, they stripped us and began torturing me. The worst torture was the electric prod -- it went on for many hours, with the prod in my vagina, anus, belly, nose, ears, all over my body. I wanted to die, but they wouldn't let me. They kept saying, 'We have all the time in the world. You do not exist. You are no one. If someone came looking for you -- and no one has, do you think they'd ever find you here? No one remembers you anymore.' The impunity they had. One would go eat, another would take his place, then he would take a break, and another would replace him.

"They kept asking me what I knew. I knew nothing. Finally, they got bored and said they wanted money. My parents somehow raised the ransom and they released me three months ago. But, I don't feel free. Those animals are embedded in my soul, what's left of it. I'm sure someone keeps their eyes on me and my family. It is an awful feeling being watched. No one deserves it."

"I saw one other pregnant woman who was kicked and punched in the head. They undressed her and beat her on the legs with something made of rubber. This lasted awhile and they carried on beating and insulting her, asking her about people she didn't know, who the father was. I saw her a few weeks later. She must have miscarried."

Cristina exhaled, nauseously. She had read similar stories: the lucky few who get raped and tortured … and are fortunate to relive the experience, every day. She knew her sister and brother-in-law probably went through something similar, or worse. She had learned that union organizers were the same as Maoists in the eyes of the national reorganization effort. It was good news to hear that people were getting out, some released with a ransom. Where she could get $5,000 was a constructive problem to put her mind to.

Cristina and Willie talked about it several times. He would document the travel details – the sights, meals, getting around – and she would meet with anyone who might know her sister. He heard second-hand stories about the torture chambers in these places, but they didn't sound real. *How do people get away with torture in this day and age?* Much was fucked up about the United States, but society generally wasn't fearful of its government. No one worried about hit squads, secret police, sanctioned kidnapping, and random murder.

"Any luck? Any leads?" Willie asked Cristina, after their long day. Willie spent the day immersed in sightseeing and colonial history and was excited to share what he learned.

"No and no," she answered. "It was awful. The girl is younger than I am. The things they did to her ..." she mumbled. "I don't know how anyone gets through it. Her story, was, um ... I don't know if I can do this. I really don't. All I can see is my sister telling her story."

Willie listened to Cristina's halting recollection of Claudia's time at La Perla. It just couldn't be true. Cattle prods and rapes and beatings, every day? What kind of people do that? She relayed her recollections of people coming and going, screaming and yelling for their lives, then the silence. Somehow, someone had put her name on a list and she ended up in this hellhole. Her story spooked Cristina. Was this really the best way to find her sister? Was it always political? Or, were these military people just extortionists? Were they chasing hopeful rumors, while the cold realities of a completely broken system unfolded in front of everyone? Was she 'disappeared' or lost in the system?

"We don't have to do this." Willie heard nothing in his three weeks back in South America that gave him any optimism. It was worse. There wasn't any force for good … or for moderation. None of the institutions did anything for its people and no one trusted anyone, except family. Argentina had become a country of scared whisperers.

"Yes, we do. We might find someone who has seen her. I can't just sit in my BA office and hope my sister is alive. I have to know. I'm fully aware that the odds of finding her are long. But what else can I do? We're headed to Mendoza, and there is a secret prison along the way called Granja La Amalia, just outside San Luis. There's a man in town who knew my sister and brother-in-law in university. He might have some information. The problem is, he doesn't answer his phone."

"We'll just keep on. We can catch the bus to Mendoza tomorrow. I have the name of someone, an American guy with USAID, to call. His name is Luis Gajate. I met a friend of his in a bar who knows my sister."

"Sounds like the beginning of a bad spy novel, but I like that he might be able to help," Cristina teased. "Mendoza's gorgeous, and the wine is wonderful. By the way, you never mentioned you had a sister. What's her name?"

"Beryl," he answered. "She got all the talent in the family. She works for a bank in New York. They finance projects across South America, so she has some contacts here."

"Yes," she teased. "I've heard her name from Alma."

"When did you talk to her?"

"Alma mentioned her name a few times."

Willie looked up surprised, although it really wasn't if he thought about it. It seemed like everyone knew everyone, and he felt left out.

Nine

Floresta, Argentina and Foz do Iguaçu, Brasil

October, 1977

"Well, when are we getting out of here to start our new lives? We better go soon, or your torturer-in-chief is going to rat on us."

Jaime knew that Marcela was right about this, but he was making money hand-over-fist for the first time in his life. Notwithstanding that Rafael Sánchez had become a huge pain-in-the-ass, sticking his nose into their business, asking all kinds of stupid, insinuating questions. He didn't respond, although he knew that his time at 3750 Bacacay Street was ending soon. He had cleared nearly $4000 in the past six months and Jaime knew he needed to leave the country before everything collapsed. Marcela made him some business cards and even opened a bank account for him in Venezuela. He was preparing for his own national regeneration process.

"Yes, I agree, the sooner the better. Sánchez is getting pretty mouthy and he's onto us. Just last week, he asked me how much money these passports go for. I told him he couldn't afford one."

Jaime looked up and sighed. "Okay, you're right. He's been particularly insubordinate lately. A real pain in the ass. He's been bugging me too."

"How about this Sunday? That gives you five days to pack up your life and get out of here. It will take me five minutes to pack my things. You took everything else."

Jaime stared back, without reaction as Marcela spoke. "Sunday morning it is. I guess we have to go?"

Marcela nodded. At this point, she was as scared as she was a year ago. He was heading in a different direction and she didn't know if he would turn her in. She heard gruesome stories of escapees getting recaptured trying to get out of Argentina, sometimes for bounties. She had grown to trust Jaime just enough, mostly through the success of their criminal enterprise. Marcela felt certain he wouldn't hurt her and she did know his new identity and everything about him. But she was completely reliant on him and he could get his hackles up, accusing her of a snooty upbringing and leftist tendencies. One week to go.

Marcela couldn't even begin to think about sleeping. Her mind was spinning in a hundred different directions, and the checklist of what could go wrong kept expanding in her head. It was three in the morning and 3570 Bacacay was silent. Herman was sound asleep upstairs and he wouldn't hear a thing. Sánchez was away this weekend, returning tomorrow morning. She had rehearsed this escape in her head over and over the past week. The bus north leaves Retiro at seven. It travels via Rosario to Corrientes and Posadas. It arrives close to midnight at the border. No one checks passports that time of night. Jaime had left an old bicycle for her, inside the back gate behind a large holly bush. She calculated the bike ride would take forty minutes. She needed to leave no later than 5:45 to be safe and she just hoped no one would stop a female bike rider on an early Sunday morning. She laughed if she could get away with saying she was going to church, particularly dressed in the threadbare nightclothes she was abducted in. So many things could go wrong, but she was excited. Marcela had not left this neighborhood in over a year. If she got caught, at least she had been free for a short while.

At 5:30 as the sun came over the horizon through the scattered clouds, Marcela gathered her modest belongings – one change of clothes, a smattering of printing equipment she wasn't able to discard and 340 US dollars. She had no pictures of Paulo or her baby, nor anything that betrayed her past. Everything she owned could easily be put in the little wicker basket on the front of the bicycle. The passport and money was all she really needed. Marcela set off toward the city on the bike. She immediately noticed two handmade signs taped to the bus shelter in front of the building. One had a black and white picture of a smiling young man dressed in a fanciful bow tie with the heading 'SECUESTRADO.' The other placard featured the banner 'DESAPARECIDA' underneath the picture of a young woman who looked to be in her twenties. The posters were dog-eared and untended, like signs for missing pets. She wondered if they were held with her at 3750 Bacacay Street, two blocks away. Three new prisoners had been brought in over the past month although she never got a look at them, being in the basement. She pedaled into town with the other light traffic, arriving at Retiro Station at 6:40 with time to spare. She bought her ticket to Rosario. From there, she needed to change busses to head north toward the Frontier.

Marcela sat in the window seat on the fourth row next to an older woman, who was going to Rosario to visit her daughter and grandchildren. The old lady was a talker, and thankfully asked little of Marcela. She had a new identity in her pocket, but preferred to listen, absorb, smile and remain anonymous. This was the first time in a year where it mattered what her name was. She had spent the past year creating new lives, including one for herself, and all she wanted now was to drift into obscurity until she safely got to Brazil. She knew she had to be smart and cautious. Anything could go wrong, but every minute she looked out of the window was a mile further from Buenos Aires.

Marcela had a twenty-four-hour head start on the Argentine police force. Unless something went awry, Marcela Rezende, the name in her newly-created Brazilian passport, would wake up in a Brazilian hotel bed the instant that *el ejecutor* arrived at work. Years ago, she took a studio art course in university from a charming Brazilian professor named Marco Rezende. He was the first Brazilian she got to know and she always liked the dramatic way he pronounced his surname. Re-ZEN-day. It sounded so exotic, particularly lingering over the 'z' as Brazilians do. She wondered if, and when, or ever, she could go back to

Alvarez or Caesares? Or was her family and married names just casualties of this endless dirty war? She never really thought about what it would be like to suddenly have a new identity. But from this point forward, she was her own creation. There was something very appealing about starting life again. Being Brazilian made her feel more exotic and youthful.

Marcela looked out of the bus window and smiled to herself a few times imagining the chaos, finger pointing, and recriminations tomorrow morning for the escapes from 3750 Bacacay Street. And most of all, the embarrassment and humiliation of losing a prisoner, a girl no less, plus the warden! She knew she must remain alert. They were coming for her, eventually. Men hate being embarrassed.

Foz do Iguaçu, Brasil

Marcela Rezende checked into the Hotel Itamaraty, a small hotel on Rua Xavier da Silva in the center of town late Sunday night. A clean room with a private shower cost $4.20 per night. She could stay here for a week, but needed to find a more permanent place to live. The hotel sat off Navy Square, across from the School of Fluviais, where inland seamen learn river navigation. The Port Authority of the Parana River and City Hall faced each other across the square. She noted the large Banco do Brasil, the Federal Police Station and Parish Church solidly anchoring the south side of the Square, next to the post office. There were small shops advertising boat and train tours of the Falls. She looked forward to the tour once she got settled in. Marcela quickly noticed Foz do Iguaçu was more of an outpost than a real city. Back in the 1930s, Brazil established a national park around the Falls and built a casino and fancy resort hotel to attract visitors to the region, only to see the laws changed and gambling prohibited a decade later. It was still a tourist destination, although there wasn't much infrastructure. There were two miles of falling water, cascading down through 275 different cataracts. Eleanor Roosevelt, upon seeing it, said "My poor Niagara." Marcela remembered hearing *ee-gua-zu* as a girl and her grandmother's pronounciation was so exotic – the Guarani word meaning 'big water.' Her nana loved reciting Guarani mythology and she remembered this distant land in the jungle. It became her goal to get here six months ago.

The first thing Marcela did on arrival was to contact her brother and sister. She spent the entire bus ride thinking through how to reach them, without getting anyone into trouble. She assumed the police had ransacked her apartment in BA and were trying to find them too. Marcela walked into a small newspaper shop and noticed a rack of postcards. She spun the stand around and selected two: one had a large bright picture of a toucan, the other, a vista of Iguaçu Falls. She paid the clerk and walked across the square towards a small café. It was easy to feel like you were in your own world here. The sticky heat and the roar of the Parana River gave the area a wild outpost feel, so different from Pando, her tidy Uruguayan home, which was wide and quiet and mostly treeless. She remembered her grandmother reading the Pachamama Tales to them as children. There was one called 'Yerba Mate,' about a mortal who saves the moon from a jaguar and was rewarded with a plant that made him alert and healthy. She thought to herself. The name of the moon in Guarani lore was Yasi. *Would they remember that? No one else would.*

That was it. She neatly copied their home addresses, careful not to smudge her handwriting onto the cards: *Having a wonderful holiday and can't wait to see you soon. Love, Yasi.* She hoped Ricardo would understand her message. He didn't check his mail often and owed people money. Cristina would instantly understand and be here as soon as she could. Unless of course, the police got to her first. Marcela's escape no doubt triggered a search.

Floresta, Argentina

Shit hit the fan that Monday morning when *el ejecutor* arrived at work to find his boss and the female prisoner gone. The artist woman's cell was clean and bare; nothing remained except an old rusted frame and a lumpy, discolored mattress. Even the pictures on the wall had disappeared. He ran downstairs to tell Jaime, but he was gone too. He'd even taken some files with him, judging by the cracked metal cabinet. His personal items were gone, everything was taken off the wall. Even his picture in the kitchen was gone.

Rafael Sánchez began to think things through. His boss and a prisoner escaped. He knew about the counterfeit passport operation in the basement. The warden and the girl were making them for the government. She printed those things out like newspapers coming off a press. He was not privy to the goings-on between the boss and his superiors, but he could swear that woman pumped out twenty passports a week. Some didn't even look Argentine.

Sánchez immediately called his superiors at ESMA, the Army mechanics school.

"What do you mean a prisoner and the warden aren't there?"

"That's what I said," he replied more assuredly than he probably should have. "I came to work this morning and everything was cleared out. Except for some printing materials in the basement."

The panicked arrival of four officers in two vehicles twenty minutes later stirred up the otherwise quiet suburban neighborhood that pretty spring morning. The men quickly entered the building and met with Sánchez, who had deputized himself as the new warden in charge. The others didn't seem to care and went about their normal start of the week chores.

"Come down here," one of the officers yelled from the basement. "They've been making passports." The small table where Marcela spent the last several months was clean and tidy. The only remaining evidence was a printer, a ream of bonded paper, and a small box of embossed Argentine passport covers. Several tubes of ink were carefully stored in a closet along with a trimmer and heat press. A makeshift darkroom was set up in the closet. "They couldn't take the printer and the camera, but it looks like they got everything else."

"That's what I told you. They may have been a couple, although I don't know why he'd want her. I had her too."

"It appears our warden is on the move. Do you have a photograph of him and the girl?" the chief officer asked, irritated by the remark. "What's the girl's name?"

"Caesares. Her first name is Marcela. Arrested in August 1976. Husband, Paulo was killed trying to escape. Union agitator from Uruguay it says here." Sánchez handed over the file. "She has a sister and brother who go by Alvarez."

"Well, I expect she has another name now," he replied. "Looks like they had a good business going. They are going to be hard to find," he said, looking at the left-behind supplies. "Did they just make Argentine passports?"

"I don't know. The woman was busy every day. I'm guessing the warden had a side business."

"They've left the country," the senior officer concluded. "I know I would if I was him. But we know their real names. And their families. Please pack this room up and go through every file they didn't take with them. We need to discourage this sort of thing."

"Yes sir," answered Sánchez. "They are traitors to national regeneration. I stand ready to help capture these criminals." He saluted the commander.

"What is your name?"

"Rafael Sánchez, sir."

The commander glared at the unkempt deputy, shaking his head. "How did this happen? Weren't any of you paying attention to what's going on? What do you do?"

"I was assigned to discipline prisoners. The artist woman who escaped was a real socialist. Spouting off on Che Guevara. Dangerous woman."

The commander looked over the file on Marcela Caesares. There was nothing that suggested that she was dangerous, or even remarkable. Her husband was a union organizer but he was silenced several months ago. The file showed that she was pregnant when she arrived but miscarried a month later. She was originally from Uruguay. The Alvarez family looked to be sympathetic to the socialists, but weren't trouble makers. The commander turned toward Sánchez. "She probably wasn't much of a revolutionary, but we need to find her."

The commander looked down his nose again at the mouthy guard. *This is what the Argentine military has become.* "It is obvious that you are not alert. That is your job. The planning for this escape was done right under your nose."

"I was in charge of discipline," Sánchez answered contritely, but he couldn't help himself. "I suspected she was trouble, but the warden assured me that he had everything under control."

"He did, you stupid idiot. He had *you* under control. This took lengthy planning and anyone paying the slightest amount of attention should have seen this coming. Roughing up a helpless woman? And a mother? You are quite the macho man," the commandant sneered.

Sánchez smiled quickly, putting his pudgy hands on his hips, standing straighter, sucking his stomach in. "I believe in discipline and the cause of national regeneration."

"Yes, you mentioned that before. I want to talk to the other guards here."

"Please be my guest," he answered. "There is a young guard who I have taken under my wing. He is very inexperienced and needs more training. There is an older man who does the cooking. He knows nothing, except football."

The commandant exhaled, shaking his head. *No wonder this country is in such dire shape with people like this.* They had to find the warden. Escapes like these were bad for morale and for his reputation as a district police commander. The girl's innocent. Seems like she just got caught up with the wrong people. But, she knows what went on here and that's a problem.

"Senor Sánchez, in light of this terrible security lapse, we plan to close this detention center immediately and transfer the remaining prisoners to another facility. But first, you need to go through everything in this building to find clues of where they went. Did they escape together? And where? People just don't vanish. Not in this country."

Sánchez nodded and he walked downstairs to the basement. He had gone downstairs earlier this morning before the others arrived. They were clearly making passports, although there was little left, except shreds of printed card stock and inks and the machines. He opened the artist woman's desk drawer to the desk. Clean as a whistle too.

He climbed the stairs and headed to her cell on the third floor. It too had been carefully cleaned. He flipped the discolored mattress on the cot and a small book fell onto the floor. He picked it up. *Bom Día, Brasil, Third Edition* by Rejane de Oliveria Slade. It was all in Portuguese. What a strange language! He couldn't understand why the biggest country in South America spoke the same language as the smallest country in Europe. But the girls were shapely and pretty, if a little darker. They weren't as pretty as Argentine women.

"Senor?" he shouted, excitedly with his find. "It appears the artist was learning Portuguese. I suspect she is headed to Brazil." He was pleased with himself.

The commandant replied, shaking his head. "Well there's only 750 miles of shared border to pick from." *Why are we detaining female artists?* Her file didn't suggest she had joined any groups. But she has stories to tell about what went on here, bad stories that can never get out to the public. If they did, a lot of people would be ruined, starting with him.

He returned to Jaime's office on the first floor, where Sánchez was combing the room for other clues of the escapees' whereabouts. "If what went on in here gets out, we're all ruined. We will be shamed. You need to find this woman? Go forth," he said dismissively, with the wave of his hand. "You can redeem yourself and your career if you find her."

Ten

Washington, D.C.

September 1977 – January 1978

Gene Propper remained irate that Orlando Bosch stood him up in Caracas. Bosch agreed to testify about meeting the Novo brothers, but then reneged at the last moment. It was that kind of case. No one wanted to confront the Chileans directly. The Agency clearly knew something, but remained vague and unhelpful. The Novo brothers identified a tall blond man, but refused to testify and a year later, they couldn't prove anything. The Cubans loved to talk, but never under oath, and didn't mind being in jail. One of them, Virgilio Paz had disappeared into thin air and not seen him since the assassination. It had been over a year since the bombing and all they possessed were scraps of information that led nowhere. No one wanted to accuse the Chileans of anything without overwhelming evidence. He and Carter Cornick still shared a small conference room at the Justice Department.

"Carter?" he asked. "Have you ever heard of letters rogatory? That's the kind of thing you UVa. people would know about. Something arcane and litigious."

"Afraid not," he answered. "You're the lawyer here. Remember, I'm the one who speaks Spanish, not Latin."

"All right, then. I've been talking with a few people at the DOJ and they had an idea." He paused, then continued. "I know -- and you and Bob know -- this was a DINA operation. We could petition the Chilean government with letters rogatory. That is a formal request from one country to another's for judicial assistance. This, in effect, is a legal summons."

The judge who signed off on the letters explained that the crime against Orlando Letelier 'was punishable under U.S. Code 1116 (a)', which protected foreign officials, and the District of Columbia Code 2401 defined Moffitt's death as murder in the first degree. 'The U.S. government,' it continued, 'identified two Chilean military men, Juan Williams Rose and Alejandro Romerel Jara, as entering the country before the crime. It is therefore requested that you cause each of these men to appear in a Chilean Court to answer under oath the written questions which are attached to this request." Fifty-five questions accompanied the document, in addition to the demand that Propper be in Chile during questioning.

"Why didn't we think of this months ago?" Cornick answered. "We've had these two Chileans in our sights for nearly a year. Why is DOJ all of a sudden being helpful?"

"Because Langley has finally decided to be helpful. Until now, uncovering the sins of Operation Condor was in no one's interest. We need to solve this case before it gets muddied again. Let's see what this mysterious American guy knows. I have a sneaking suspicion people in our government were aware that DINA was after Letelier. They just didn't have the imagination to believe good allies would blow him up in the middle of Washington, D.C."

"Well, " Propper smiled. "This letter rogatory also gives us permission to leak this whole hypothesis to the press. That is our only ally. You watch how quickly the Chileans give him up and blame Langley for Letelier's death. Their press has been looking for an opportunity to get back at Pinochet for censorship."

"Can't they just deny it? We know that no one with those names came into the United States prior to the murders."

"They could," Propper answered, somewhat impishly, "but we have photographs of them from the passport applications through Paraguay. Chile doesn't know that. We could leak the pictures of these two mystery men to the press. We owe Jeremy O'Leary at *The Star* a scoop. Let's try it to see what comes back. It could be a dead end, but official channels have been useless. We've got nothing to lose."

A week after the publication of the names in Chile produced no one, *The Washington Star* ran the story with the photos across its front page, including a threat that the U.S.

government was ready to sever ties with Chile. The photos were wired to newspapers around the world, requesting assistance in identifying the two officers. Immediately, *El Mercurio*, Santiago's leading newspaper, reported that 'Juan Williams' resembled Michael V. Townley, a North American electronic technician resident in Santiago from 1970.'

Propper's boss, Larry Barcella called him. "Have you heard about Juan Williams?"

"What about him?"

"Then, you haven't. You're too calm," said Barcella. "Are you sitting down?"

"Yeah, I'm at my desk," answered Propper. "What is it?"

"They identified Juan Williams down in Chile, Gene. The blond Chilean turns out to be an American named Michael Vernon Townley!"

"What? How do they know?"

"It was in *El Mercurio* yesterday," explained Barcella. "People are going crazy in Santiago. A lot of folks seem to know the guy. He's a fuckin' American." News of the letters rogatory letters hit the front pages of the *Washington Post* and the *Washington Star*, then ran on NBC, ABC, and CBS. It was the first public acknowledgement that Washington was focused on Chile in the year-and-a-half-long investigation. Questions were immediately raised in the world press and diplomatic meeting rooms: Why and how did Townley, son of a senior Ford executive in Chile, become a mechanic? Who did he know in the U.S. government? Was he CIA? Who ordered him to kill Letelier? How did these men obtain diplomatic passports to travel to the United States in 1976?

As soon as Townley's name was made public, agents at the Justice Department and FBI began assembling physical evidence against him, including records of calls made from his sister's home in Tarrytown, New York to a Mexican restaurant in New Jersey, where CNM members were known to congregate. Townley also called Guil Novo from that number, two days before the assassination. The FBI also found evidence that Townley bought pagers and ingredients for the bomb at local stores in Westchester County. The puzzle was coming together.

The Dirección de Inteligencia Nacional sent two agents to the United States in August 1976 via Asuncion, Paraguay to murder Carlos Letelier, although only one, Michael Townley, arrived on U.S. soil. Through Townley, DINA hired several members of the Cuban Nationalist Movement to assist in the assassination. For eighteen months, Propper and Cornick chased down leads to nowhere and crazy gun-toting Cubans dressed up like women. Now the tall mysterious character had been identified: an American living in Chile.

Propper and Cornick got on a plane to Santiago, after the Chilean government announced that they would produce 'Williams' for questioning. "They'll have to release him, he's ours," Propper argued. "He's the key who can link the Chileans presumably responsible for commissioning the murder of Letelier with the Cubans." It took six days for Chile to produce Townley and he answered only six of the fifty-five questions sent by the D.C. grand jury, invoking his rights against self-incrimination. He denied involvement in the Letelier-Moffitt assassination. Propper knew they had to get him out of the country before he fled, or more likely, was 'disappeared.' Townley's American citizenship partially solved a problem for the Chileans: by turning over Townley, Pinochet could claim to have cooperated with the United States, while being vindicated that no Chilean was involved.

The optimism vanished the next day. Scherrer, Cornick and Propper met with Odlanier Mena, the new head of intelligence, to iron out the transfer details of Townley's departure that evening. "Two weeks?" cried Propper. "That is totally unacceptable. I'm not waiting two weeks. The fundamental fact is that this man is American. He is wanted in the United States. He's in this country illegally on a false American passport. So, he is ours. The other issues are irrelevant. You give us Townley, and then we'll discuss everything else without all this pressure."

"You have to appreciate something, Mr. Propper," Mena answered slowly. "The President believes that we run worldwide propaganda risks if we hastily turn Townley over to you. The Marxists of the world will criticize Chile for bowing to the forces of United States imperialism."

"What's that got to do with anything?" Propper answered. "Why should you care what the Marxists say if you are doing the right thing?"

That evening, President Pinochet held a news conference. "I've said this before. No one, I repeat no one within this government of Chile bears any responsibility in the Letelier case. We are doing everything possible to get to the truth and see that those responsible are punished, whatever their position or nationality." The next day, two other stories appeared in *El Mercurio* detailing how Chile complied with the Letters Rogatory and that two Chilean agents had nothing to do with the assassinations. There was no evidence that Pinochet planned to release Townley to the Americans.

Propper and Cornick were outraged. "Frankly, I don't believe your people are trying very hard," they accused Mena. "I hoped we wouldn't get to this, but Mr. Townley must answer the U.S. government's questions. Or," they continued, "all U.S. relations with Chile will be endangered. This could mean a complete halt in trade, loans, investment and diplomatic relations."

Another week passed. Once again, Cornick and Propper, now joined by Bob Scherrer, continued to meet with top Chilean intelligence officials and expressed the 'extreme urgency that the US Government attached to the immediate expulsion of Michael Vernon Townley.' The conversation had turned to arcane legal appeals over deportation, when the French doors to the meeting room opened and in walked Pinochet.

"Please continue, don't mind me," he instructed his advisors, while he paced behind their chairs. Then Pinotchet blurted out: "We were doing so well, so well, ready to take off. And then this! This is a banana peel, senores!" His voice was hoarse and tired, his carefully parted hair and trim mustache sat heavily atop a dark uniform. He had a scowl on his thick face and the stare from his pale blue eyes was cold and weary.

"A banana peel!" he repeated. "If we step on it, the government will fall. We will fall!" He walked out of the meeting as quickly as he entered, leaving the participants grasping for a fuller translation. Scherrer looked across the table at Propper and Cornick trying to suppress a smile. Townley was finally theirs if they heard him correctly.

The final agreement was signed that afternoon. A year of stonewalling had been cleared away and Pinochet was finally cutting his losses. Chile would expel Townley if U.S. prosecutors promised to keep any information about DINA activities -- other than the Letelier-Moffitt assassination -- out of the press and from other governments. Propper also agreed to say nothing about the agreement itself. At seven a.m. the next day, Scherrer was in his Santiago hotel room, brushing his teeth when he received a call.

"Get out to Pudahuel Airport right away," said the caller, who didn't identify himself.

"Townley's lawyer is maneuvering. He's booked on Ecuadorian flight 52 to Quito scheduled to leave at nine-fifteen. We need to get him. Don't worry about tickets and reservations. We'll take care of that. Please hurry,"

Scherrer called Propper, "Gene, we have to take the risk. It may be our only chance to get him. These people are slippery." Forty-five minutes later, Scherrer and Propper arrived at Pudahuel, where airport authorities had delayed the flight, concerned that Townley might be planning to escape to Quito.

"Mike," Propper began, after Townley was handcuffed and taken from the plane. "You understand, don't you, that you are in deep trouble and you will be arrested as soon as we reach United States soil?"

"I didn't think you were taking me on a picnic with these bracelets."

At this point, Propper didn't know what role Townley had played in Letelier's murder, or how the bomb had gotten under the Chevy Chevelle. He suspected the American was a courier between DINA and the Cubans. The DOJ's evidence against Townley was thin. They could prosecute him on passport fraud, but little else. If he refused to talk, they didn't have a case. The Cubans had managed to keep quiet for a year-and-a-half.

Cornick put Townley in a window seat and sat down beside him. Once airborne, he showed Townley the warrant and said he would be arrested the moment the plane touched down on American soil. "You can make this easier on yourself if you come clean."

"I know how you feel, Mike," said Scherrer, leaning across Cornick from the aisle seat. "Your own people have betrayed you and kicked you out of the country to face this all alone. You don't owe them a thing."

"You have no idea what this means," Townley said numbly. "There are still all kinds of Christian Democrats buried inside the government. If Pinochet goes, they will take advantage of it to push for a return to a liberal government. And the Marxists will be right behind them. I guarantee it."

"Mike, we don't know anything about that one way or another," said Cornick. "Our job is to solve the Letelier case. That's why we came after you."

Townley's face hardened. "You can't prove a thing."

"Let's not talk about it now," Scherrer answered. "This isn't the time or place."

Hours later as the plane crossed over the Caribbean Sea, Scherrer tried another tack. "Mike, I can tell you've been in the intelligence business for some time. So, have I. All right?"

"If you say so."

"We discovered that I know some of the same guys in Argentina that you do," said Scherrer. "Same places too. You know the Café Tortoni?" Townley just looked ahead silently. "And I know the CNM guys too. I was kicking

Iggie Novo's ass in New York ten years ago. So, we both know Cubans."

"Maybe so," Townley answered.

"I'm not trying to get anything out of you now," said Scherrer. "What I want to do is to talk to you as one professional to another. We're going to have a long, miserable flight if we can't trust each other, and we have to go with you every time you take a piss."

Townley nodded. "Where did you grow up?"

"In a lousy section of Bedford-Stuyvesant in New York," Scherrer replied. "With a crime rate you wouldn't believe."

"Well, I didn't have anything like that," he answered. "In Iowa, I used to go to an old-fashioned ice-cream sundae parlor with my father and have chocolate sundaes. He and I used to mow the lawn together back in the early fifties. We had one of the first big power mowers back then, and he rigged up a pulley system so he could support me while I pushed the thing on the steep banks of grass. I had a very pleasant life until I was thirteen or fourteen."

"Until you got to Chile."

"I guess so," said Townley. "Everything changed then."

Two weeks later, Miami police pulled over a grey Lincoln Continental with expired license plates. An inspection of the vehicle found a Derringer pistol, a .45-caliber automatic, two .38 caliber Smith & Wessons, a weighing scale, a large plastic bag full of cocaine, birth certificates for several people, and another bag containing wigs and disguises, mixed in with $30,000 in cash. Amongst several fake IDs in the driver's possession, police noticed one for a 'Guillermo Novo.'

"Mister Novo?" the agent at the Miami FBI office began, "or, should we call you Victor Trinquero? Or Alvin Ross? Or Virgilio Paz? Whoever you are, you're in a world of trouble. In addition to the items we found in your possession, we have a warrant for your arrest for violating probation. You are not allowed to leave the New York metropolitan area. I've been told to tell you that Michael Townley is also under arrest. You and your brother might have met him in New Jersey, back in September 1976. Name ring any bells? He's tall and speaks with an American accent?"

Michael Townley had been confined at the Fort Meade Army base, when Cornick and Propper visited him a week later. "Now it's every man for himself, " Cornick told him. "The rats are leaving the ship. Your partner got sloppy and got caught with $30,000 worth of blow. That's penitentiary time, my friend. He'll say anything."

Townley looked up, surprised. "I don't do business with drug dealers."

"Please, Mister Townley. No need to burnish your credentials for us. You, of all people, should know that these men are unprincipled individuals who deal in unlawful activities to support themselves between their mercenary contracts."

Townley smiled wearily, realizing it was over. "If I don't deal, I'll go to prison for entering the United States with false passports, at least twice, seven years per entry. You'll give me fourteen years?"

"Yep," said Cornick. "And that's before we get you for the murders. Which we will. You left quite a trail: telephone calls, receipts, you name it. Plus, these Cubans can't keep out of trouble. They keep dealing drugs and blabbing. Mike, this whole thing is collapsing. We'll spare your wife in Chile," he added. "What do you say?"

Michael Townley signed an agreement with the U.S. attorney to give his full testimony. He pled guilty to one count of conspiracy to murder a foreign official. He would not have to discuss any DINA activities outside the Letelier case. His sentence would be no more than ten years in prison with the possibility of parole after three years and four months.

Propper, Scherrer and Cornick were happy, although there was no celebration. They had only gotten one of the foot soldiers for the killings. There were others.

Eleven

Foz do Iguaçu, Brasil

November, 1977 - January 1978

On her third day in Foz do Iguaçu, Marcela met Eduardo Maloof as she was mailing post cards to her siblings. "What a fresh vision of loveliness to brighten this ordinary space?" came a baritone voice from behind her in line at the post office. Marcela turned around and smiled at a short, husky man in a rayon shirt and bottle-thick eyeglasses. Others in line giggled. She was not yet fluent in Portuguese, but she liked his poetic lilt, a *visão de beleza,* 'the vision of loveliness' Marcela turned and smiled shyly at the man. It had been a long time since she'd been paid a compliment by anyone, much less a man.

The odd little man continued. "This is a frontier town. Beautiful females rarely come here," he announced as others, including two women in line, smiled nervously. He looked comfortable talking loudly and openly to the crowd. "Welcome fine lady and new face to the Triple Frontier.

You do not look like a tourist. I can spot the tourists. My name is Eduardo, Eduardo Maloof. Everyone knows me." He extended his hand and slightly bowed his head.

From the smiles and head shakes, it appeared to Marcela that his boast was accurate, at least among the city's postal customers that morning. She immediately liked Eduardo, although she demurred from introductions in the middle of a post office in a foreign country where she was cradling a counterfeit passport. She made eye contact, smiled and nodded her head.

A week later, she noticed Eduardo and two men in military uniforms walking purposely through the square toward the bank. He waved to bystanders as though he was the town's mayor, off to do important civic business. She kept her head down, turning her face away. Marcela was irritated at her sloppiness. She had left her Spanish-Portuguese translation book at the prison. *Relax,* she told herself. *No one will find me here.*

Marcela learned of a small rental cottage outside of town from the hotel owner. The owner was sympathetic to her financial predicament and wanted to help this new person in town. No one could remember the last single woman who moved to the Frontier. The cottage was located downstream from the dam, about four miles north of town out on the edge of the national park. It was owned by the funny little man who introduced himself in the post office. "You've seen the owner around. Can't miss him. He's a Syrian or Turk or something. He owns half of town. It's got great views of the river. He rents it off and on," the hotel owner said, with a wry smile. "Whenever he feels like it."

"I can't afford much," she lamented. "I'm an artist. I paint portraits of people if you hear of anyone looking," she laughed. Marcela had a modest cash reserve from her passport forgery proceeds, but knew it wouldn't last her long. She wanted to get back into painting and the cottage had a view of the Parana River.

The owner of the hotel mentioned that she could make a decent income selling artwork at the local galleries. "Everyone wants a momento of their vacation to Iguaçu Falls. Something to put on their wall at home."

"That's great news. So, how would I find this man? What's his name?"

"Eduardo Maloof. He's worth knowing and not crossing. His family owns half of Foz. You know those industrious Arabs?"

"He introduced himself at the post office."

"He's quite a character. A good spirit for this town."

"He has an office across the square," the hotel owner continued. "You should pay him a visit. He likes new people moving to town."

Marcela wasn't sure about renting a cottage from this stranger, who she heard also traded in light firearms and counterfeit goods. She was flattered by the attention Mr.

Maloof had paid to her in the post office and she figured she needed a few friends in this alien land. What did she have to lose?

No. 234 Rua Bartolomeu de Gusmao was a non-descript building behind the bank. It certainly didn't look like the headquarters for a real estate mogul. A disinterested heavyset woman sat at a desk, reading *Contigo*, a celebrity gossip magazine. She glanced up.

"I was wondering if Mr. Maloof is in? I don't have an appointment."

"I'll check. *Eduardo*," she yelled loudly.

"*What?*" came a muffled irritated reply.

"*Someone's here to see you.* What's your name?"

"Marcela Rezende," she answered quietly. The woman yelled her name through the closed door. There was no reaction.

Marcela smiled. "Okay, how about "*a visão de beleza?*"

A short, stocky man peeked around the door frame. "I knew you weren't a tourist," he beamed. The receptionist continued reading the magazine, making no move toward politeness. "Please come in and don't mind her," he said, motioning Marcela to the door behind the receptionist.

"Would you like coffee?"

"Thank you," Marcela nodded.

Eduardo Maloof's office was piled high with everything imaginable – folders, papers, books, velvet artwork on the wall, a Guarani headdress made of parrot feathers, and several ceramic bowls. The office was cramped and the wallpaper was tattered and yellowing. Whatever his source of income was, he didn't spend it on fashionable interior decoration. There were books of law on a side table and rolls of drawings and real estate plats sat heavily on a large chest of drawers that dominated his office. "Forgive the mess. I've been meaning to clean up, but I've been too busy. I remember you from the post office. How can I help you?"

"I just moved from Florianópolis and am looking for a place to live. The owner of the Itamaraty mentioned you have a cottage that you rent."

"Possibly," he smiled. "What are you prepared to offer?"

Marcela's face drooped. He had used the word *oferecer* which she thought had sexual connotations. She'd had enough of men wanting things from her. She stood and began to turn toward the door. Eduardo looked up, surprised. "I didn't mean that kind of *offer*. Heavens, no! What I meant is what are your requirements? It's very cozy, hardly big enough to be a studio. What is your budget? Do you have a car? It's five miles out of town."

Marcela sat down, exhaling, still agitated. "I'm sorry. I don't have a car and I can only afford $75 a month. At least until I can find a job. I'm looking at a car next week. I'd like to be in the country, out near the falls."

"Well, well," he answered. "We can figure these things out. What are your job skills? People move here for all sorts of reasons. But there needs to be some basis for trust and understanding of what you can afford. I can tell from your accent that you are Argentinean, probably from Buenos Aires. You are not from Florianopolis with that accent and bone structure. You're from a good family, of Spanish not German extraction. I can see that in your hands and your ears. Small ears are a product of good breeding. Look at me with my big jugged ears. Common as pig tracks."

Marcela laughed. "Actually, I'm Uruguayan by birth." She relaxed. "But you are right. I came from BA. I don't plan on going back. You asked about my skills. I'm a painter, but have learned from necessity to put my skills at composition to a more practical use." She wanted to tell him the whole truth. He had warm eyes and a gentle smile and she wanted to open up to someone after all this time. But Marcela couldn't be sure. The stakes were too high. "How did you end up here?"

"My family was in the textile business in Damascus. We moved to Sao Paulo when I was a teenager after the military coup in the late-forties. My father knew many Syrians who came to build the dam and we moved here in 1960. A far cry from the Levant. My only complaint is the humidity." He smiled. "And other traders, of course. The Triple Frontier is a very entrepreneurial place and I'm always looking for a set of skilled hands. I come from a

intricacies and subtleties of Portuguese, Paraguayan, German and U.S. passports. She was not nearly as efficient as she was working under Jaime, but that was OK with Eduardo. He lived closer to town and often went across the bridge into Paraguay, where most of his clients operated. "There's a plastic surgeon on the corner just as you get off the bridge, who 'reimagines' people. If one doesn't like being a big-nosed Argentine, he can give her a cute button nose and a new nationality, too. Ain't this world great!" he laughed with a wink. "Everyone can have a new start."

Marcela enjoyed Eduardo's eccentricities and generosity. He occasionally brought her trinkets from across the river, if only as mocking celebration of their new home. Last Friday, he presented her with an oil painting on velvet of the Marina Piccola on Capri island. Two weeks earlier, he had brought her a bottle of ten-year-old aged Scotch whiskey made in Paraguay. Typically, Eduardo crossed the Friendship Bridge on Friday with his passel of passports and envelopes with documents for his other businesses, returning late in the afternoon. His price – usually $100 per – was high, but no border agent had ever flagged one of his products, so business was booming. Eduardo had a smattering of other business interests across the river that he rarely discussed with Marcela. There was a good high end select market for IWI assault rifles from Israel ('the best, from the best') and Swiss SIG-Sauer automatic pistols ('you won't lose a duel with one of those').

Unflaggingly polite and friendly, still no one dared to cross Eduardo Maloof. He was reportedly the largest private land owner in this part of the Parana state, but he possessed an informal bearing of just another short, pudgy local merchant. He waved to everyone and they waved back. He asked about family and children always, whether to the grocer or a competitor. He mostly tinkered with cross border money laundering and smuggling, if only to keep the pulse of the frontier and to see who and what was coming and going. He was always looking for land to buy. Eduardo blamed it on his homeless middle eastern upbringing. "I got tired of wandering the desert and wanted a permanent home that no one could take away from me." Passports were a side line business, but one he enjoyed keeping his fingers in. "You never want to be stuck here. Always remember that smart Brazilians put their money in banks, not *bancos*," he laughed. "Maybe one day these generals realize that they're making it worse? Open up the economies, take off the tariffs and let unfettered capitalism shout from the rooftops. Thus far they haven't figured out what motivates people. Money and progress."

Marcela enjoyed her regular exchanges with Eduardo. He had taken her under his wing and respected her privacy. Eduardo never married, which at first seemed strange to her, until she realized he was permanently engaged to his various businesses, referring to them casually as 'his sons.' There were vague whispers about his light arms trade, although Marcela never asked and he never felt the need to explain. These were off-limits topics that seemed completely appropriate to a resident living here.

Twelve

Buenos Aires, Argentina

January 1978

Nearly six weeks had passed since Marcela Caesares' daring escape from 3750 Bacacay in Floresta. With the exception of finding a Portuguese translation book, there was nothing left. Rafael Sánchez removed what files he could on the Alvarez family before they closed the facility down. The commandant gave him little direction other than to 'find the girl.' He knew that his superior really meant to *silence* the girl. Marcela Caesares escaped to Brazil, he concluded. Finding her would be close to impossible. But what about her brother and sister? *Surely, they know where she is?* Everything about the Alvarez family was right on his lap. He looked out of the window as the municipal train slowed entering Retiro Station, then again at the sheaf with their files.

Brother: Ricardo Alvarez, age 24, resides at Jose Marti 3406, Pocitos Beach, Uruguay. No known political affiliations. Occupation: Unknown

Sister: Cristina Alvarez, age 28, resides at Paseo Colón 741, Depto 3, San Telmo, Buenos Aires. No known political affiliations. Occupation: Architect

Rafael Sánchez didn't care much for Buenos Aires. It was crowded and everything was expensive. He needed to find this artist woman's sister. The artist had a brother too, over in Uruguay. He pulled the map from the inner pocket of his uniform as he exited the station. Pedestrians gave him wide berth as he waddled down the Avenida 9 de Julio. It was a half-hour walk and Rafael liked admiring the large monuments along the wide thoroughfare. *This is a powerful country worth fighting for and protecting,* he thought to himself, heading south toward San Telmo. He noticed a group of women in the square holding up signs and chanting names. What is this? He walked quickly around the square, muttering about socialists getting what they deserved.

He looked again at the note in his pocket. Paseo Colón 741, Depto 3. He stared at the simple apartment building, stepped up to the front door and rang the buzzer on Apartment #3. There was no answer. The shades on the windows on the third floor were drawn. He buzzed #6 and #2 as well. No one was home. Finally, a female voice came over the speaker.

"Who is it?"

"We need to leave tomorrow. This is why we are here." Cristina stated. "I'm almost certain. It has to be Marcela. It just has to be her."

"It's a long way and who knows about the Argentine police," Luis added. "They keep very good records. When they kidnapped your sister, they wrote down every piece of information about her. Her name, where she lives, family history, everything …"

"Including …?" Cristina jumped in.

"Yes, I expect they know about you, too. Do you have other siblings?"

Cristina's face dropped and she stared at Luis. "I have a younger brother who lives in Uruguay."

"Can you get a hold of him? I'm sure they are looking for both of you. No loose ends with these guys."

"I can try to call him."

"No, that's not a good idea," Luis answered. "Any friends we could call to alert him?"

"I'm not sure," she answered. "He was working to open a bar or something. I have his address, but we don't keep up that regularly."

"Who knows where you are?" Luis asked.

"No one," Cristina answered anxiously. "Except a neighbor who forwarded the card and some bills. But she wouldn't tell anyone. Porteños know what these policemen are like and what they can do."

"Well, let's hope so," Luis answered. "Remember these policemen have the complete support and resources of the Republic of Argentina behind them. And I suspect they'll want to make sure she doesn't tell the world about her imprisonment. Very few people get out of those places alive. She must be resourceful."

Cristina grimaced. "My older sister is tough. Tougher than me or my brother." Her face turned serious, thinking about him. "How can we warn him? He's a bit of a free spirit. Never listens to anyone."

"It might make sense that someone checks in with him. I have a few friends in Montevideo if that helps."

Cristina looked over at Willie and smiled. "I'd appreciate anything you can do to help us."

Luis copied down the information into a small notepad. "This is helpful. My guess, based on everything, is that she's made it to Brazil. She must have gone there with fake identification. The Argentine police have her real name. They could cross the border if they have a solid lead, but no one wants to get in a shooting war over an individual," Luis continued. "People are desperate. No one trusts anyone, and certainly not the government. We don't have much influence. It's a carrot and stick relationship.

"… And we're still providing them with sticks."
Cristina didn't like America – the blind opportunism, the
ignorance, the consequences of both for ordinary
Argentines.

"Yes, and a few carrots. And grapes. Don't forget
grapes." Willie was happy to lighten the conversation and
ordered another bottle of Malbec. It was an evening for
news and celebrations. Marcela was alive. And he'd just
learned that he and Cristina needed to get the hell out of
Argentina as soon as they could.

The postcard gave everyone hope, but the discussion
about meticulous government record keeping made
everyone aware that they were at risk. The endless stream
of Malbec only made the discussion more emotional. "The
Argentine army is looking for me and my family. My sister
may -- or may not -- be in Iguaçu Falls. You have a plane
ticket and a passport out. I'm stuck."

She was right, of course. Young Argentines were stuck.
And Willie did seem to have a pipeline of guardian angels
handing him off one to another, like a golden baton at a
relay race. His sister must be somebody important to have
that many people looking out for him. It had been a
stressful three months for Cristina and she tried to keep her
emotions and expectations in check and to maintain a clear
head. They were preparing to drive a thousand miles to
find her sister and flee Argentina, her home and a place she
used to love. Willie couldn't imagine being run out of
America for doing nothing. "It's not as though I'm some
sort of seditionist … or spy. How can we live in such a
place?" was her final pronouncement at 2:25 in the

morning. She had gotten into the cigarettes at that point. Luis had smartly bid them farewell a few hours earlier and headed home. He would check with a few people in the morning in Montevideo to see about Cristina's brother.

Before departing, Luis gave Willie a contact. "Ken Wells is a friend who's up there working on the dam," he smiled as he wrote down his name and telephone number. "He goes by Ziggy and he's a piece of work. He's sort of a sentry for U.S. interests who has worked all over Hell's half acre. He understands these big infrastructure projects, where we need to have eyes on what's going on. I'll ring him in the morning."

"Don't tell me? Is he another friend of my sister's?"

"More of a friend of a friend, but I've learned it's good to have friends," he laughed. "Latin America is very relationship-based and trust is hard to build, particularly now. There are people in certain places in the world that people just know. He's one of them. Your sister is too."

Willie had to laugh. This was an efficient cohort. At every turn, his sister seemed to have watched over him.

Kenneth 'Ziggy' Wells was a native Georgian with thick hands and a red expressive face. At 6'2'' and 225 pounds, the tropical climate left him perpetually in a lather and often out-of-breath. He was a running back on the 1952 Georgia Tech national championship team. Wells was a force of nature, an outdoorsman who some would say had gone native. Everyone called him 'Ziggy,' for the quick feet that allowed him to zig-zag on pulling trap plays.

"Don't just stand there, come in and shut the door," she laughed. "And remind me how to do this." Cristina had taken most of her clothes off and stood beside her backpack at the edge of the single bed. "This will be interesting," she said. "And, certainly memorable in this small bed."

Willie sat on the bed and put his hand behind her head, stroking her dark hair. "I've always wanted to run my hands through your hair. You have great hair. It's wilder and thicker than when we started."

"Dirtier too. A hazard of life on the road," Cristina said, touching Willie. "And you have blond hair. Something Argentines see rarely, unless it's dyed. And that's mostly the women." She began kissing him gently, still figuring out the choreography in a single bed, before they fell into each other. They had hugged, but never caressed each other before.

It was almost nine and they needed to get up, finish packing and go to the rental car agency. Cristina was still asleep and Willie was lying next to her, thinking how their relationship took a dramatic turn last evening. The conversations had gotten emotional after the second bottle of wine and things went from there. They argued half the night before and after sex. It was a well-deserved hangover. He hoped hers wasn't that bad, but she barely looked alive, splayed across the tiny bed. Willie's head was throbbing, but he was excited by the new possibilities and destination ahead. They were headed to Brazil.

"Are you alive?" Willie teased, shaking her arm gently. The evidence wasn't clear.

"I think so," she answered, rolling over. "Did we sleep together last night?" she asked, coming to.

"Yes, we did," Willie said, taking her hand in his. "You showed me some new things and we both appear to have survived."

"Good. It was overdue. I thought I'd forgotten how."

"Me too," he answered awkwardly, not knowing where to take the conversation. It wasn't as though he had lots of anecdotes to relay. Willie liked that she joked about it and took it on as her first conversation of the day. He wasn't quite ready for that. "I'm going to pack and get the rental car. Meet your downstairs in an hour? I need to call Luis this morning about a guy he knows up at Iguazu. He works on the dam."

"Yes, I vaguely remember. A CIA guy? I think I went off the rails at that point." Cristina had pulled the sheet down. "I'll pack up, take a shower and wash my hair. You remember, 'washing that man right out of my hair?' from *South Pacific?*"

"I like your hair. I think we talked about it last night."

Thirteen

Points North, Argentina

January 1978

The landscape rolled on monotonously, punctuated by small towns. Luis had discouraged them from travelling by bus or train. "They might have Cristina's name posted. They don't know you. Rent a car. It suits your reason for being here. You know the travel guide?" In all the excitement, Willie forgot that he was there to write a travel guide. They had thoroughly researched Cordoba and Mendoza, but with the arrival of postcards, the purpose and itinerary of the trip had changed. They weren't writing a tourist guide any longer.

Willie's headache eased as he finished a third cup of coffee that he bought a half hour earlier. 'Night Fever' came on the radio. An amped-up DJ began babbling and Willie leaned forward to cut the radio off. Cristina was still sound asleep. She looked just like a little girl, all tucked up into herself, but she had a scowl on her face as she slept. The one thing Willie couldn't do is sleep in a ball. He needed to stretch out and he could never really sleep – or read -- in cars anyway. Willie was still sorting out that they slept together last night. Was everything different now? Or not? Cristina didn't seem concerned that their relationship changed earlier this morning.

When he wasn't analyzing their relationship, Willie fantasized about his sister's hocus pocus world on the morning ride north. He'd enjoyed spending yesterday with Luis, his sister's business associate. Willie always wondered what a spy looked like. He assumed George Smiley, with code names, aliases and midnight cigarettes. But Luis Gajate looked like he got plenty of sleep and wasn't particularly secretive. They drank a lot of wine and Luis voiced his opinion on the dirty war, the cynical generals, and the burgeoning drug trade to the north. What a wild job being sent out as a re-con man for the U.S. government! He thought about all of his experiences over past four months and where they were going now and why. The book was writing itself.

Willie pored over the checklist of literary themes in his head that he remembered from an English course in college. *Love? check. Death? check. Good and evil? definitely. Coming of age? embarrassingly, yes. Power and Corruption? yep, have that in spades. Survival? hopefully. Courage? hers not mine. Redemption? yep that too, maybe.* Willie Thomas was driving north on an empty Argentine highway with a hungover successful architect he had just slept with in route to find her sister who had escaped from a torture center. That's what he was doing on this ordinary Sunday morning and all of a sudden, Willie began to feel important and good about himself.

Cristina stirred, her puffy eyes opening, trying to focus on the remainder of the drive. A light dry breeze blew through the window. "Was it a bad dream? Or was I smoking a cigarette last night?"

"Perhaps both," Willie answered. "We all had too much to drink. But it was nice to have something to celebrate. Let's keep it going."

"I haven't had a cigarette since I was at university. Serves me right." She stirred, sat up and looked over at Willie. Her face was flushed and her mat of unruly hair flopped against the window. "And just to confirm, we had sex twice last night and it was fun. I should space these indulgences out."

I've just slept with the most exceptional person I've ever met, he thought to himself as he quietly watched the landscape go by, listening. Willie turned on the radio. Barry Manilow's 'Copacabana' came on. *His name was Rico, he wore a diamond* … "I can't handle this," he said, shaking his head.

"Makes me think of my brother," she laughed. "I wonder if he got a postcard? I loved the Yerba Mate story my grandmother used to tell us as kids. Ricardo paid no attention to Nana's folk tales."

They stopped at a gas station outside of Rio Cuarto. Willie wanted to get to Santa Fe by late tonight. It was a quiet Tuesday morning and there was no traffic on the road. He gulped down another cup of coffee and ate a stale croissant and continued north. Willie worried what they were going to do if they didn't find Marcela in Foz do Iguaçu. Then where? Turn around? If they found Marcela, then what? He'd head home to write his expose on the Dirty War? What about Cristina? Could she stay there with her sister? Or come to the United States? Willie passed a sign, 440 kilometers to Santa Fe. They were making good time.

Willie's mind drifted onto what's next. What was he going to do? He still didn't know. And now his relationship with Cristina had changed everything. Argentina was vast and uncrowded, but he knew they had to get out of the country. The police knew the family names now, and no doubt would track leads until they found Marcela … and them. Get the family together and take it from there. Cristina had dozed off again.

He looked up in the rear-view mirror, thinking he heard a sound. Willie's heart sunk as a boxy sedan with a red light on its roof came over the crest of the hill. Cristina stirred and then jumped as the siren sound got closer. Willie checked his speed. He was only going 110 kilometers an hour. He took a deep breath and pulled the car over to the side of the highway.

Willie felt as uncomfortable as he could remember. His heart was pounding and his queasy stomach returned. He tried to take deep breaths and exhale, but that just made him dizzy. Cristina stirred and looked in the rear view mirror. "Let's hope he's in a good mood. Make sure you smile and be polite. Stay cool and friendly."

The baby-faced policeman approached the stopped vehicle on the side of highway 14, twenty miles south of Posadas. "Licencia y registro, por favour."

Willie handed the young man his passport and rental car information. The officer returned to his vehicle and began talking on his two-way radio. A minute passed, then another. The longer he sat there in his car, the more anxious Willie became. After a few minutes, the policeman got out and approached the car.

"What is the purpose of your visit to Argentina?" he asked officiously.

"Estamos buscando una guía de viajes," Willie answered in stilted Spanish, handing him a crisp business card.

Cristina immediately took over the conversation. "Señor, estamos escribiendo una guía para que los jóvenes estadounidenses visiten Argentina." The policeman smiled, but looked confused. He handed Willie's passport back to him. "May I see your identification, ma'am?"

"Certainly," she answered cheerfully. "My friend and I are traveling all over the country to research a travel guide for international visitors. We are planning to see several of the World Cup qualifying games. We will be returning to Buenos Aires in June for the final matches."

The policeman nodded his head, excitedly. "I like Americans and American football. But nothing is like Argentine football. And we are again the favorites to win."

"My friend likes the Dallas Cowboys, *the gauchos*," she laughed, pointing to Willie. "They just beat the Broncos in the Super Bowl last weekend. Or I should say they beat the *caballo cimarron*."

Everyone laughed. The young policeman was enjoying the exchange, and he weighed in on the tournament and Argentina's chances with their new sixteen-year-old hotshot midfielder, Diego Maradona. He wished them safe travels and returned to his vehicle. Willie looked across at Cristina, who wore a big grin.

"I've learned that most men instantly forget what they are talking about when the subject of football comes up. Plus, there's really no need for him to know who I am. I'm just a passenger, now without a country to call home. Only one more day, and I'll be free of this god awful place." Cristina looked again at the map and the Fodor's guidebook. They were still three-and-a-half hours from Santa Fe. "It looks nice. It's right on the Parana River and there are four cathedrals in town so we can pray about getting out. There is a hotel called the San Martin in the center. Rooms are $16 with a private bath. Let's get going before he remembers that he forgot to check my ID."

"When did you become an expert on American football?" Willie asked. "You've never expressed any interest in sports, much less American sports."

"I have no interest in football. I just noticed an article in the *Herald Tribune* this weekend about the Super Bowl."

Over the past three months, Willie and Cristina had been inseparable, but spent most days apart. It was a comfortable relationship and they had a calming effect on each other. She pursued contacts who might have known her sister, while Willie collected brochures and kept notes on where they were and what he was noticing. The rhythm of their days came together each evening over dinner, before they parted for separate bedrooms. Those had been the ground rules Cristina established back in September when this all started. Happily, that had changed.

After a daylong hangover, eleven hours in a smelly rental car, a successful interaction with a football-loving policeman, they were exhausted. Cristina dozed off again, curled in her little ball. Willie began to recount how this whole thing started. His father had been bugging him to get a job. He was going for an interview in the District and the Chilean secret police set a car bomb off in Sheridan Circle. Willie remembered the rain and the traffic jam coming home, then talking with Alma about her life in South America. He wondered about the role chance plays in life. Everything he'd done since last September 21st was because of Orlando Letelier's murder. He looked over at Cristina, her face pressed against the window. How on earth does she sleep like that? He looked ahead as they entered the central plaza in Santa Fe, the pleasant little river city, and saw the sign for the San Martin hotel.

Cristina got out of the car, stretched and walked towards the front door of the hotel. Willie grabbed their backpacks from the trunk of the rental car and walked toward the light over the front door.

"How many rooms, senora?" the desk clerk asked Cristina as she looked around the plain threadbare lobby.

"Just one," answered Cristina, without looking over at Willie. "We've had a long day driving and wondered whether you have a quiet room off the street." The clerk handed Cristina the key as Willie dragged their backpacks through the lobby and up the staircase. They smelled of sweat, coffee, old wine, dust, cigarettes, and leaded gasoline. Last night things changed and now their relationship was completely different.

Willie and Cristina slept through the night, curtains drawn, exhausted from their lengthy drive. They lay in bed like rag dolls, both sprawled across the full size bed, occasionally hearing a car horn, realizing their plan of getting up early had gone awry. Cristina got out of bed and opened the blinds. *Where in the hell are we?* She crawled back into bed and pulled the pillow over her head. Willie assured her that her name wasn't on any nationwide all-points bulletin. They could relax and sleep all day, they deserved it. In the afternoon, they took a short walk on the promenade along the Parana River, before the sun disappeared. Neither of them were hungry, nor particularly gung-ho to look around another provincial city with a plaza, a river, a park by the river, and three cathedrals. They returned to the hotel room and had sex again before falling into a deep coma. It was another all day drive tomorrow to Iguaçu.

Cristina's spirits and color returned the next morning and she began thinking about her sister. There was momentum now to their journey and she spent a good part of the day imagining when and how she would run into her. Luis said that Iguaçu was a small place in the middle of nowhere so they were bound to run into one another. Cristina was still cautious. They were close, but anything could go wrong and the thought that someone might be chasing her was always on her mind.

The landscape changed as they headed north toward the Falls. It was warmer and the trees were taller and more tangled. "Let's see, today we shall be clear-headed tourists," she began enthusiastically. Cristina pulled out their dog-eared *Fodor's* guidebook and began planning their last day of driving. "We may want to bypass these sights, but there is a mate museum along the way if that is of interest. Pray to the deity of Yasi. There are the usual ruins of Catholic missions and a huge metal cross in a place called Santa Ana. There also is a little German town and a little nature preserve. We just keep following the Parana River north." Willie smiled and looked over at Cristina. Her hair was pulled back as a breeze blew through her window. She looked so free and alive. It was nice to think of Cristina as 'his girlfriend.' "I also found a hotel in town called the Itamaraty," she continued. "Suits our budget, particularly now that we are sharing a room." She winked at Willie.

Fourteen

Washington, D.C.

January – March, 1978

The trial began on the sixth floor at the U.S. District Courthouse a few blocks from the Capitol on a snowy day amid extremely tight security. Several of the witnesses were put under federal marshal protection, due to numerous death threats. Bomb-sniffing dogs prowled the halls and forty-five news organizations, including thirteen from Chile, trudged through a metal detector at the entrance to the building, then were again searched and identified a second time before entering the courtroom. The courtroom only seated sixty people, so there were tussles and arguments on who could enter the court and who could sit where. Riot police surrounded the courthouse. *The New York Times* noted that 'the supporters of Letelier tend toward shaggy hair and rough loose clothes. They long to lead the poorer nations of South America away from the capitalism espoused by the junta headed by General

Augusto Pinochet.' The Cubans, meanwhile 'seldom affect casual dress.'

Guillermo Novo and Virgilio Paz faced charges of conspiracy to murder a foreign official, murder of a foreign official, first-degree murder of Orlando Letelier and Ronni Moffit, and murder by use of explosives. All five counts were punishable by life imprisonment. Paz remained a fugitive, and was thought to be hiding in South Florida. The government charged Ignacio Novo with two lesser counts: perjury before the grand jury and failing to report a foreknown felony. According to the indictment, the Novo brothers and Paz helped Michael Townley organize the assassination and obtain the lethal explosives. Townley was not indicted with the Cubans, but was permitted to plead guilty to a single count of conspiracy to murder a foreign official.

The Cuban Americans in the audience remained defiant. Novo's daughter yelled to the press entering the court, "The government has nothing. They have shit. They won't be able to prove anything because they rely on that degenerate Townley. He has no country, he has nothing and he would sell out his own mother." Paz's brother-in-law was also in the audience, who despite his indicted fugitive brother's absence, sat among the spectators threatening the gathered press pool in the rear of the courtroom that "nobody will neutralize or stop us in our struggle against communism. For now, we are biding our time watching this trial. But if it doesn't go our way, then you will hear from us." Threats continued through the trial. The father of one witness received a call from Ignacio Novo, who didn't bother to conceal his identity. Novo

made sure the slide switch on the bomb was on, secured it with the last of my duct tape and re-joined Mr. Paz and Mr. Novo. I reminded them to detonate the explosives whenever Mr. Letelier was alone. They either didn't listen or did not care.

"I drove north to New York City late that night, before flying to Miami, then back to Santiago. I informed Mr. Pedro Espinoza that the mission was a success. He relayed that his superior and 'conveyed his satisfaction by smiling."

The Novo brothers whispered in Spanish, shaking their heads, their voices becoming louder, as Townley delineated the complex plot. "Faggot." "Watch Your Step." "Traitor." "Degenerate CIA shit." "Son of a Whore." A Cuban woman sitting with them shouted "Cortarle de lengua! Se disparan palomas taburetes!" ('Cut out his tongue, Stool pigeons are shot!") Judge Barrington Parker grew aggravated and quickly demanded silence from the defendants and their supporters.

Michael Townley never reacted to the taunts, his monotone voice describing every detail of the plot. He went on to outline his reimbursement for 'their direct expenses incurred during the operation itself. It was sent to Mr. Virgilio Paz and Mr. Guillermo Novo in the early weeks of October 1976. The sum did not exceed $1,600."

Paul Goldberger, attorney for the Cuban defendants, jumped in. "Your honor, the defense believes that Mr. Townley should be fully interrogated about his participation in the assassination of Carlos Prats in Argentina and the shooting attack on Bernardo Leighton in

Rome. We have documentary evidence of Mr. Townley's presence in those countries at the time of the attacks."

"Your honor, the prosecution objects," prosecutor Larry Bardella replied. "Mr. Townley has agreed with the prosecution that he could only be required to testify on crimes in the United States, or against United States citizens. As a public servant and agent of DINA, he was released by the country of Chile to only discuss Letelier in all its ramifications."

Judge Parker waved his hands, cutting off the debate. "The plea agreement is valid. I will not allow you to cross-examine the witness with respect to the Argentine and Italian incidents."

Propper continued to lead Townley through the plot to kill Letelier and now asked him to identify exhibits to back up the oral testimony. An array of items, including passports, drivers' licenses, motel and gas station receipts, highway and restaurant tabs, airline tickets and photographs were entered one-by-one into the record. Townley slowly took the courtroom through physical evidence including wires, plastic cups, electric matches and how they, when put together, had served to kill Orlando Letelier and Ronni Moffitt.

"You needed an insider," Propper concluded. "That's how you find out what happens inside a conspiracy. Without Michael Townley, this monstrous crime never gets fully solved, does it? … And, without that agreement, Michael Townley wouldn't testify … and all of the co-conspirators would escape." It was an admission that

Townley had, in effect, become part of the prosecution's team and that he was able to define the terms of his own testimony. He refused to answer questions about the internal workings of DINA and about other crimes he committed in its service. Most importantly, he protected Augusto Pinochet.

The jury retired to render its verdict. After eight hours, the jury forewoman stood and read the decision without emotion. Guillermo Novo: Count 1 – Guilty. Count 2 – Guilty. A litany of 'Guilty's' followed charge upon charge. The same for Ignacio Novo and Virgilio Paz, in absentia.

The defendants sat stone faced, as friends and family began to sob. One family member shouted at Judge Parker, "Nigger. Black son of a bitch" before he was restrained. Ignacio raised a clenched fist and shouted "Viva Cuba!" Then, he looked at the reporters with a quizzical smile and a shrug, saying quietly, "The dice came up craps."

The trial was over.

Guillermo Novo and Virgilio Paz in absentia were sentenced to consecutive terms of life imprisonment in a maximum security institution, with eligibility for parole in 1999. Ignacio Novo was sentenced to eight years imprisonment for perjury and misprision of a felony. Michael Townley, in accordance with his plea bargain, was sentenced to ten years, with credit for time already served. He was placed into the federal witness protection program with a new identity and was confined to an undisclosed medium security prison, being eligible for parole in October 1981. At the sentencing hearing, Townley again expressed no remorse for killing Letelier and said he hoped to return to Chile to live after serving his time.

In the nine months following the trial, the Cuban Nationalist Movement defiantly continued its battle by murdering two exile leaders who had advocated reconciliation with the Cuban government and by carrying out six more bomb attacks in the New York and Washington, D.C. areas. Their cause would continue.

Fifteen

Foz do Iguaçu, Brasil and Points South

February - April 1978

Marcela developed a familiar rhythm which made her content. She enjoyed sitting on the screened-in porch with a cup of tea listening to the nightly orchestra of wild things in the canopy above, along with the steady rumble of water. Elis Regina was singing 'Águas de Março' on the shiny new hi-fi with all sorts of knobs and dials. Marcela admired the Brazilian pop singer, particularly after she called the military junta 'gorillas' in a Dutch newspaper. A large toucan had taken up residence in a nearby palm tree, no doubt happy to have a new friend to feed him and voice to compete with. Other glamorous birds brought their plumage and exotic calls to the neighborhood, mostly in the morning. She furnished her cottage simply and cheaply, and the tacky gifts from Eduardo were happily displayed on the empty walls. He bought her a Van Gogh last week over in CDE, protesting that he had no wall space in his office. Marcela usually spent two days a week at the Falls doing watercolor and pastel drawings for the tourists and three days forging Brazilian, Spanish, and American passports.

She and Eduardo came to an agreement: she would work for him, if he gave up his lucrative Argentine passport business. He agreed to forego that business to his competitors and perhaps even introduce a pang of guilt into the counterfeit community. "You can have them as clients," he told them. "No more for me. I'm done." That's what he and Marcela agreed on. Business must have a conscience in the Triple Frontier.

Late in the afternoon, Marcela was heading through town to the post office and noticed a young couple sitting across the main square. They must be tourists, she smiled, noticing they looked more seasoned. The man facing towards her was definitely American, she guessed by the khaki pants and boat shoes. She looked again and saw a woman sitting across from him who looked like her sister. She had a straw hat and sunglasses on, so it was hard to tell. The woman picked up her fork with her left hand in a way Marcela had seen thousands of times. That awkward elbow out that plagues all lefties. Her hair was tousled, but it was definitely Cristina. Marcela approached the table cautiously, circling the pair from a distance, still not trusting her eyes, wary of making a scene. "Cristina?" she whispered with quiet excitement, as they gasped and jumped up from the table. They began hugging and twirling in a circle, tears running down their faces. Willie rose and greeted this stranger, remembering the pictures of her they studied four months ago. To Willie, it all felt surreal.

Quickly they pulled back, cautiously looking around, as Cristina wept. Caution now was an essential behavior. They smiled and lowered their profile, giggling in disbelief, I cannot believe it is you. "It worked. I can't believe it worked," Marcela said, out of breath, "You got the postcard."

"We got the postcard. We got the postcard," was all that Cristina could say. "Come, let's go. I have a car now," she chuckled, motioning her hand, warily looking around the square. "You won't believe this but I am living here with a new last name. *Rezende*," she purred out. "Something fittingly Portuguese. It's a long story and I can't wait to tell, you. I can't believe you are here."

The bumpy ride toward Marcela's cottage in her 1970 Ford Maverick reminded everyone why she moved to the city and didn't get a driver's license until recently. "It's rugged," she laughed as Willie sat in the back seat, surrounded by their bags. "But peaceful. We all need peace right now."

"Amen, sister," Cristina seconded, as 'Night Fever' came over the radio. "I like these Bee Gees. You'll have to ask Willie about disco. He went to one in Montevideo with Ricardo."

Willie chimed in. "Yes, we heard that song at least fifteen times on our drive up. It's catchy."

"I sent a card to Ricardo, too. I don't know if he got it." Marcela chuckled at her joke. "What do you think?"

Pocitos Beach, Uruguay

Ricardo Alvarez noticed a brightly colored postcard in his mailbox with a picture of waterfalls and a toucan. It was postmarked 'Foz do Iguaçu, Brasil. 18 deciember 77.' He'd never been there, but he'd followed the news about the construction of a huge dam on the Parana River. Excavation began a few years ago to divert the seventh biggest river in the world. It was going to take decades to build. The handwriting looked familiar, kind of artistic, done in blue ink, but the card wasn't signed. All that was written on the back was his name, address and the name 'Yasi.' He didn't know anyone called that. What kind of name is *that*?

Ricardo's newest plan to open a restaurant had bounced around. Doing business with restaurant people was always a challenge. He finally found a new partner, but the guy was a big talker and *visionario*. Everyone had interest, but no capital to invest. Ricardo was no economist, but trying to raise money in this environment was fruitless. Not to mention the hyperinflation and currency devaluation that made U.S. dollars the only money anyone would trade in. He might as well get into the pharmaceutical business, full time.

He unlocked the door to his apartment on the Ramblas, thinking about the card, shuffling through the rest of his mail. *Who did he know there? And who is Yasi?* He shook his head. Name sounds familiar, but he couldn't place it. The handwriting was precise and stylish. *Both of his sisters printed like that*, he thought for a second. *Could it be*

236

Marcela? No that wasn't possible. He put the mail on the kitchen counter, just as the phone rang. It was Juan.

"Do you owe anyone money?" he asked.

"Well, good day to you, too," Ricardo answered. "Of course, I do. What's going on?"

"A policeman came around earlier looking for you. What have you done now?"

"Nothing. At least, recently."

"He looked like trouble, asking about you and your family. Something about your sister. Definitely a cop or paramilitary. I'd get the hell out of town if I were you. I told him you've been out of town, but I'd relay the message. He said not to bother. Consider yourself warned." Juan hung up.

Ricardo knew what the uniform meant. The man was looking for Marcela. Now he's looking for me. The handwriting on the card. The card itself. Could all of this be related? Maybe she escaped from the place they were holding her? He had to sort this out quickly, but he was still foggy from last night. He took a deep breath. *First things first: A uniformed man is looking for me. I need to get the hell out of town, head to the border.* Who else might send him a card from Iguaçu Falls? No one he knew had ever gone there. Why would they? He thought for a second, *Marcela must have escaped and now they were after her ... and him.* He looked at the road map he kept in a drawer in the kitchen. It was six hours to the border with Brazil. Then another full day north to the Falls. Ricardo's mind was racing. *If he was nosing around the bar, he must know where I live, too. Fuck!* Suddenly, Ricardo was panicked. He quickly looked around his apartment. *What do I take?*

He ran into his bedroom and pulled out a suitcase. Ricardo's mind was spinning. He glanced out of the window of his apartment. He didn't notice any strange cars on the street, but then again, one never does these days. He looked into his full closet and shook his head. Ricardo would need several armoires to pack up all his clothes, but he had to go, now. He reached in and grabbed several shirts, four pair of his best Haggar's, underwear, a second pair of shoes, and three pair of socks and threw them into the bag. He looked out of the window again. Nothing new. Good. He reached into the back of his dresser drawer to a small carved wooden box. He counted out his savings. $900 U.S. dollars in crisp twenty-dollar denominations. He stuffed the money into his bag and zipped it up.

Ricardo Alvarez spent a very quiet, but restless night at the Brazilian border town of Jaguarão. There were more direct routes to Foz do Iguaçu, but this got him out of Uruguay quickest. Another full day on the road tomorrow and he would be there, although Ricardo wasn't completely sure where 'there' was. The border crossing that he was dreading turned out to be unmanned, so he celebrated in a seedy highway hotel room with a Brahma beer and his last line of cocaine. Ricardo could read Portuguese, but had trouble understanding it spoken. Brazilians were so theatrical in conversation, speaking with a lilt, their vowel sounds longer and wider and enunciated, with sentences often ending in upspeak. Ricardo listened carefully to the desk clerk extruding her words in suggesting a place for dinner. She recommended a churrascaria on the main square called do Magro, which had the best barbeque in the entire state of Rio Grande do Sul.

That was one thing about Brazil that always bugged Ricardo. They were the biggest and best at everything. He was raised in the world capital of the finest beef, but always had to listen to Brazilians bragging about how good their damn beef was. Worse than the Argentines. Same as in football. The sumo wrestlers of the continent. World Cup was coming this year and he looked forward to his country's chances. Like everything else about Uruguay, finer days were in the past. After upsetting Brazil to win the 1950 World Cup and finishing fourth in 1954, lean years followed and by 1978, Uruguay was no longer a world power in the sport. But, their beef was still the best in the world.

"Boa noite," he smiled entering the restaurant, his pronunciation garbled as though he was chewing a dinner roll. Portuguese was hard for him to speak and understand. The waitress smiled, wondering what this dashing young man was doing here on a slow Tuesday night. He must not be from these parts, she thought, eying his flared pants and open shirt. "Uma caipirinha por favor?" he asked politely.

"Sem problemas," she replied, smiling, amused by this diner's outfit. Business had been slow this evening, so she lingered and chatted, wondering if this natty Uruguayan guy was much of a tipper.

An older man in a toque shuffled out of the kitchen with an enormous skewer of meat. "Picanha?" he asked.

"Sim," Ricardo answered. "E uma taça de vinho tinto, um malbec, por favor."

She nodded, "Obrigada," and disappeared back into the kitchen.

Ricardo was finally settled in. He looked forward to a steak, a caipirinha, and a glass of wine in whatever order she brought it out. The drive had been long and monotonous and he was tired. Tomorrow, he would drive all day to Alta Cruz. Then, another half day into Iguaçu Falls. He hoped that this journey was worth it. The stories about Ford Fairlanes coming in the night were part of a national nightmare for young Uruguayans and Argentines. It was as though the grim reaper had come to fetch you in a very unstylish car. If Ricardo Alvarez was going to die, it sure as hell wasn't going to be in a Ford. He didn't understand how this all had happened so quickly. Life used to be so normal. And now, it wasn't.

"Another caipirinha? Or a glass of wine?" the waitress asked. Ricardo was tired, but nodded. "Just a glass of wine, thank you." After this he would go to bed, get up early and head north to Iguaçu. He wondered what he would see when he got there. It was a hasty decision to just go, but every Uruguayan his age knew the consequences of staying if the police were after you. That handwriting was his sister's, although he didn't understand the reference to Yasi. Who in the hell is Yasi? His sisters had their own language. It will work out fine in a few years, he told himself. Then, I can return when this government gets kicked out.

Two years ago, things were great. The Uruguayan economy was roaring. People were out spending money. Then the government announced a currency change. Ricardo didn't understand why the 'peso' was now called a 'nueva peso' and there were 1000 of them for every 'old' peso. And the new peso was made up of 100 centesimos. It was hailed by the Uruguayan politicians as a good move for the economy, although Ricardo never understood the argument. More for less?

Southern Brazil

Ricardo Alvarez was on his way to the Triple Frontier. He was headed to Iguaçu Falls, but there was no need to rush now. After the night in Jaguarao, Ricardo looked again at the map. He had planned to head northwest toward Cruz Alta, but noticed that Balneário Camboriú was up the coast. He'd heard of it -- the poor man's Rio. There was an enormous statue of Christ on a mountain overlooking the city and the beaches had the same grand sweep with a black-and-white tiled promenade as Ipanema and Copacabana. That it was a sister city to Punta del Este made it an irresistible stopover. *It's a day's drive, but what else do I have to do? I was so close to that deal out at the beach, too. It'll be there when I get back.* Ricardo never realized things had gotten so bad that they were hunting down people like him. He had no taste for socialism. Can you name anyone who ever saw a well-dressed Russian? Those people literally kill for blue jeans.

The promises of pretty girls and beaches were too tempting not to take the short detour. It was a full day's drive up the coast, and the weekend was coming. He wasn't quite sure yet if he was suited to inland river life. The Rio Plata was more of a bay, its width nearly 140 miles mile at the mouth and Ricardo enjoyed the seasonal rhythms of beach life. Foz will be a good landing spot until things calm down and I can go back home to enjoy Uruguay's 300% inflation rate, he snickered to himself. How many beautiful women would he meet in the jungle where there were snakes and jaguars and caiman? He wanted to check out the bars along Avenida Atlantic to get some ideas for his upcoming venture and maybe, meet some locals. Ricardo was sure there were places that had wet t-shirt competitions, and word had it that Brazilian women are beautiful -- and loose. Much better than the talent at The Disco Bar.

Ricardo took the exit for 101 at Pelotas and drove north along the coast just as 'Grease' came over the radio. The sun was shining and both windows on his Fiat Uno were rolled down. Six hours to go and Ricardo began planning his well-deserved weekend. World Cup fever was spreading throughout the region, as the tournament was starting in June. Already there was controversy. Dutch star Johan Cruyff, the Golden Ball winner from the prior World Cup, announced he wouldn't take part, because of the 'dirty war.' 'The Argentines will find some way to cheat and win,' Ricardo answered the radio announcer. 'They always do.' Comparisons to Hitler's 1936 Olympic Games were frequent in the international press, further irritating the already prickly Argentine junta. Right now, Ricardo wanted nothing except a big weekend with lots of parties and dancing. He owed himself that after being run out of Uruguay. If he knew he was headed to a beach, he would have brought along a few more slacks and another pair of shoes. He should have brought the new huaraches, they'd be perfect for beachcombing, but he forgot. Too much on his mind, as usual.

The city appeared in the distance like Oz. Glistening modern high rise structures rose out of the sand along the shoreline like a space age erector set. The statue of Christ atop Morro da Cruz appeared to be holding a giant sombrero, adding to the city's offbeat ersatz feeling. Ricardo needed to find a cheap pousada for two nights. With any luck, he would be sharing it with a female he'd yet to meet. The tourists strolling along Avenida Atlantic looked prosperous and solid. He didn't notice any of the dirty street urchins that accompanied any visit to Rio. He'd gone there with friends a few years ago and was pickpocketed. He liked this better. Balneário was an enormous seaside theme park, without a hint of menace. He kept waiting for Mickey and Minnie Mouse to pop up from a beach chair to welcome him to town. Maybe this is what Punta del Este could be? One of Ricardo's skills was 'imagineering', a term he liberally used when discussing any sort of development deal.

Ricardo spotted a small pousada on his way into town. It appeared clean from the street and rooms with a private shower cost eighteen reais. It was worth checking out. He was tired from the lengthy drive, but excited for the weekend. He pulled into the parking lot in front of Vila Atlântica Antiga, gathered his bag, and entered the hotel. A tall young man sat behind the desk and greeted Ricardo. "Olá, boa tarde."

"Olá, você tem algum quarto?" Ricardo asked.

"Sim nós temos um quarto de solteiro com chuveiro por 18 reais," he answered. "O Melhor valor no balneário."

Whether or not it was the best value in all of Balneário was an open question, but the hotel had a vacancy. The hotel clerk was friendly and solicitous and the pousada was located two blocks off the ocean with free parking. Ricardo handed the clerk a twenty reais note. "What are the best discos in town?" he asked.

"I personally like the Lit Bar or the Duo Lounge," he answered, with a knowing smile. "Best scene, best music. Post Tropicália, MPB, Jovem Guarda, outre tempo. Both are just up the beach," he continued, pointing vaguely out the window north. "They really don't get going until after midnight. It's a party town on the weekends. Enjoy yourself."

This was music to Ricardo's ears, although his knowledge of Brazilian music was scant. He remembered the bossa nova craze from the 1960s and the girl from Ipanema, but that was old folks music now. He liked the Tropicália style, although he didn't much understand it. It sounded exotic and Ricardo looked forward to the evening. It was just after six, and the sun had begun to set behind the Cristo Luz. He could take a short nap and grab dinner before the evening fun.

Showered and ready, Ricardo set out walking along the beachfront promenade. It was a far cry from the lazy, laid-back vibe of its sister city. The desk clerk, who introduced himself as Marco, was friendly and told Ricardo about a seafood restaurant a few hundred meters along the praha.

The buildings were modern and tall; space-age structures sprouting from the wide arc of beaches stretching north. He had changed into his evening outfit -- high-waisted flared denim jeans and a plaid ruffled shirt – and strolled along the tiled walk. The breeze felt refreshing and it was good to stretch his legs. The clerk mentioned that it would be easy to score coke, ludes or poppers. "Everyone in there will be high and dancing," Marco mentioned matter-of-factly. "Or even having sex in the bathrooms. As I said, it's a party town."

The spirit of John Travolta's strut in the opening scene of *Saturday Night Fever* bounced through Ricardo's mind. He hoped for a score to enhance the weekend. The idea of sex in a bathroom, or stairwell, or really anywhere intrigued him. He considered himself a connoisseur when it came to the ladies, although he was never *that* adventurous. *These Brazilian women must be nuts*, he thought to himself happily, imagining the orgy he was about to be in.

The Lit Bar wasn't quite up to its name at 9:30 p.m. that evening. Marco said it would be dead that early, but soon he'd be out of gas without some stimulants. The space was huge, but empty with three enormous balls over the dance floors, spraying colored light flashes over the cavernous area. The disco was as big as a high school gymnasium and had the same number of dancers as the first hour of a middle school prom. Ricardo approached the bar and ordered a caipirinha, still thinking about his upcoming drug and sex orgy. He was open and ready for business.

A handsome man, sitting on a stool next to a woman at the bar, turned to him with a smile after he ordered his drink. "Where are you from?" he asked in Spanish. '¿de donde eres?'

"Your sister city," Ricardo answered with a swagger, as the couple looked puzzled. "Puente del Este. I own a restaurant. I'm meeting with some businessmen about investment opportunities."

The couple smiled, slowly turned and stared at the overdressed guy. "Where's Punta del Este?"

"In Uruguay," Ricardo answered, hurt. "On the Rio Plata, across from BA," he threw in. "Fantastic beaches."

The couple nodded, smiled quickly, then turned away from Ricardo. He sipped his drink, surprised at their rebuff. The Lit Bar had become more crowded over the past hour. There were several couples dancing to 'Boogie Oogie Oogie' as Ricardo began to tap his heels to the music. He expected a warmer welcome and assumed by the accent that this couple was Argentine. They could be so snooty. Uruguay was laid-back, easy-going and surprisingly wealthy and sophisticated. 'Little Wonder.' Everyone knew that, he reasoned. Or they should. Maybe Puente de Este needs a marketing campaign? The Rio Plata really isn't a river. It's more of an ocean bay. Visitors need to understand that too.

After his slight, Ricardo's mind turned to staying awake longer and having sex. He was exhausted after the ten-hour drive, but the caipirinhas had given him a lift. Two men in their twenties took seats at the bar next to him. One, with natty teased-hair and a large moustache, was dressed in an off white pantsuit and his friend looked several years younger. He was gangly and wore a tight tee shirt and jeans and barely spoke a word. Ricardo wasn't sure about this pair, but the older guy seemed friendly.

"I'm on my way to Sao Paulo for a business meeting," he fibbed. "Thought I'd stop in to check this place out. I own several bars in Uruguay."

The two men seemed excited to talk to him, their eyes brightening as Ricardo expanded his story to include other whoppers, like partying with the football players on the national team. Ricardo kept going, regaling tales of coastal misbehaving. With each and every sentence, he became a bigger and more important player in Puente del Este ... wherever in the hell that was.

"Care for a popper?" the older man asked, offhandedly. Ricardo had tried amyl nitrite only once and it kept him up for hours. He always preferred cocaine, but he knew beggars couldn't be choosers.

"Thanks," Ricardo answered. That was the nicest thing he'd been asked in a while.

The evening continued into the morning, with the three men leaving Lit Bar at 5:30, just as the early sky began to warm and brighten the continent. The trio went to a hotel room, where cocaine was offered (and accepted) and finally (and thankfully) the evening ended after Ricardo declined to participate in a threesome.

The remembrance of the older man asking him to join him and his boyfriend had been bugging Ricardo ever since he woke up at three in the afternoon. The sun finally found a way to penetrate the pousada. *I didn't see it coming. Whoa! Two guys began making out on the sofa in the hotel suite. Then the one with the moustache took off his shirt and motioned me to join them in the bedroom. Fuck. I ran away into the bright sun with people jogging and doing calisthenics along the promenade. Now it's already getting dark again.*

A quiet night and I'll leave first thing in the morning. This place is nuts.

Ricardo woke the following morning, still shaken by his encounter. He still felt dirty after two lengthy showers. He didn't see it coming. Bar people have a sixth sense and understand come-ons if nothing else, but his antennae had failed him. Ricardo was still trying to piece together how he wound up in a back alley hotel with two queers doing cocaine. Was he that desperate? Had he gotten to be a drug fiend? He needed to get on the road and get away from this twisted seaside theme park. Foz de Iguaçu was a full day's drive ahead. It would take him at least that long to erase the experience from his mind. He'd seen some shit in his day, but this was something else. It would take time to heal and Ricardo remained agitated.

He turned on the radio. "Waiting for the End of the World' seemed to be an appropriate song. He liked Elvis Costello and there was a lot of new music on the radio, much of it coming from punk rockers in England. They certainly didn't dress for success with all their piercings, work boots and stupid hairdos. Who ever said a Mohawk was flattering? Ricardo could never understand why anyone would stick a needle through the skin of their nose to affix a ring. What are they? Cattle? Why are their shirts always ripped? What was up with these freaks? Punk will never succeed here.

He smiled at the lyric from the song, 'the legendary hitchhiker says he's knows where it's at, Now he'd gonna go to Spain, or somewhere like that. With his two-tone Bible and his funny cigarettes, his suntan lotion and his castanets. Waiting for the end of the world.' Still, he couldn't shake the worry that he might come over a hill and get flagged by the police. He felt safe now in Brazil, but Ricardo had to start thinking about what he was going to do when he got to Foz. $840 in savings wasn't going to get him very far. Hopefully this period will be over soon, Ricardo thought to himself, and then he could go back to Uruguay after he finds his big sister.

Ricardo had always looked up to Marcela. She was the oldest and the first of the family to move across the Rio Plata to Buenos Aires. Everyone was so proud of her. During her third year at university, Marcela brought home a handsome man to meet the family. Paulo was tall and rangy with long sideburns, who believed in the cause of the poor. They were a free-spirited couple and Marcela always encouraged Ricardo to follow his dreams. Never a conventional student, he took a job after high school bartending and waiting tables at a popular bar along Pocitos Beach. The seasonal job became a year-round assistant manager job and finally, he had some 'walking around money' as he liked to call it. Ricardo was not a planner nor a saver, so most of his proceeds had gone up his nose. He also invested in a new venture backed by Juan at the Disco-Bar. They were really close on this idea of a chain of Uruguayan steak houses. "Uruguayan beef should be its own brand," he argued to would-be investors. "You know like Russian caviar or Swiss cheese. We should own the high-end steak house brand niche. Argentina is so mass market."

Ricardo pulled into town late. It was after ten and the center of town was silent, except for a pub on the corner. On closer inspection, there was an Italian restaurant on the Rodoviaria that looked open and a small hotel called the Fortaleza on Rua Barbosa had its light on. He drove up the square and parked. "Do you have a room?" he asked the clerk, an older man who smelled of stale tobacco.

"Yes, this is a hotel. Of course, we have rooms," the man answered, shuffling towards him. Ricardo thought he might have just awoken the man or that he was hard of hearing. "A single is eight reais, with a shared bath. Singles with private baths are twelve," he relayed grumpily.

"Well, I'd like one for a week. With a private bath. Any discount for longer stays?"

"Fifty reais for the week. You look like a trustworthy sort, but I'll still need half up front."

Ricardo was still mumbling to himself about having to pay half up front when he walked out of the hotel the next morning. He was not counting on that, but the hotel was central and he didn't have a timetable. He was here to find his sister, however long it took. Sooner or later, everyone runs into one another in a place as small as this. He planned to inquire at the post office, but he wasn't even sure what to ask. Marcela might have changed her name when she came here. *Excuse me, do you have a resident named Yasi? She might live out at the Guarani Indians resettlement,* he chuckled. That name and story had come back to him on his drive north and he now knew Marcela had sent the card from here. In the meantime, he would nose around and get to know this town. He wanted to give this restobar on the far corner a look too. It specialized in casual food like pizzas, and 'hamburguesas.' Tomorrow, he would take the tour of the Falls. This place had potential.

Ricardo awoke at 9:15 the next morning to the sun piercing the slatted blinds of the Fortaleza. The humidity had already begun to cling to his skin. Foz was small with an eight to ten square block city grid. He entered the travel agency, advertising tours of the falls in the front window.

"I'd like to take a tour," he said to the young woman behind the ticket desk.

"Next tour is in one hour," she said, pointing to the red canopied toy train just outside. "It leaves from the track over there. That will be two reais."

Promptly at ten, the narrow-gauge train engine hooked to six small carriages and, with a few toots, climbed up the paved grade. Ricardo noticed monkeys in the trees jumping between limbs and howling at one another. The conductor was speaking Portuguese over a tinny loud speaker, as Ricardo stared out at the unfolding lush landscape, enjoying the peace. The little train motored up the path through patches of clouds, past short glimpses of cataracts with rainbows glistening in the sunshine. Ricardo got off with the other passengers at the top of Devil's Throat, a horseshoe-shaped fall that cascaded 300 feet into the mist. Ricardo was already waterlogged from the humidity and spray as he walked along the slippery path down the hill. He noticed a few vendors, under umbrellas, selling flowers, paintings, sketches, even a few Guarani headdresses and cartons of British 555 cigarettes. He noticed a slight woman with her back to him sitting alone under a big straw hat, sketching a young girl with pastels. He couldn't see her face, but there was something in how she was sitting with her chin out that Ricardo remembered.

At that instant, the woman under the hat looked around and noticed a familiar man with a familiar walk in a loud Dacron shirt coming her way. "Oh my God," she screamed, squinting through the mist, then jumping up from her chair. "It can't be. It's you, *hermano bebe*," the woman said lunging towards her brother. "You made it. You got my postcard and you made it, too." She hugged and hugged him, twirling around on the pathway amongst tourists in raincoats. The eleven-year-old girl having her portrait done looked on in puzzlement at the grown-ups jumping up and down like winners on a game show.

"You won't believe it but Cristina arrived three weeks ago with Willie, the American you met last year. Remember him?"

"Of course. Well, sort of," Ricardo answered excitedly. "Let's just say we had a big night at the Lit Bar. I can't believe all of us are together."

"Well, you must come stay with me. Cristina and Willie are staying too, at least for a few more days until they get settled in and figure out what they are going to do," she waved towards her brother, writing her address on a paper bag. "I wouldn't have it any other way. All of us together," she said. "I need to finish up this pastel for my customer over there," she said pointing to the woman with the cute child being drawn. "Give me fifteen minutes. We've got so much to catch up on."

The reunion of the three Alvarez siblings was a teary affair for the initial twenty-four hours. Everyone just hugged everyone else and cried. Willie made himself scarce by going into town to buy groceries and run errands. The family simply enjoyed being together for the first time in over a decade, recounting childhood tales from asados in Pando. Marcela was seven years older than Ricardo and moved to BA for university. The only thing he remembered was a gentle hippie who made cool tie-dyed and silk-screened T-shirts. Marcela recounted her escape from the prison outside BA, but hadn't yet shared anything about her yearlong stay there. All they had learned was that she was held in a large four-story military building in the middle of greater Buenos Aires. Cristina and Willie had been staying on the sofa in the cottage, until they figured what they would do next. Ricardo's four-day sprint to Iguaçu had left him tired and without a future plan. Now what?

Over dinner that night, Ricardo caught his sister up on the beach scene along the Rio Plata, including his latest and most promising business deals that had been interrupted by a policeman looking for him.

"What did this policeman look like?" she asked.

"I never saw him," answered Ricardo. "My friend said he was fat and wore an irregular uniform. That was enough for me to pack up, get in the car and head for where the postcard came from."

Marcela paused, turning her head as if to align a flashback. *Fat with a sloppy uniform? It couldn't be. What are the odds?* It wasn't time to alarm her brother, but she had a sick feeling in the pit of her stomach.

Sixteen

Foz de Iguaçu, Brasil

February, 1978

It was a very straightforward project. The dam would take ten years to build and made sense for everyone, except the poor Guaranis. They'd be picked up and moved somewhere else and given a few reais for their trouble. Getting these countries to work together was the real challenge. Brazil was bankrolling the project, with Paraguay donating most of the land. Brazil needed the electricity. Paraguay, with one-tenth of the population, needed neither the dam, nor the electric power. Paraguay was the most isolated country in South America, run by an army general who declared a 'state of siege' when he took over in 1954. The novelist Graham Greene once referred to Paraguay as 'an island, surrounded by land.' These neighbors were mismatched from the start. One hundred years earlier, Brazil and Paraguay fought a war that wiped out two-thirds of Paraguay's population, including 90% of the country's men.

It was always smoother working for strongmen, however repulsive they were. Ken Wells had worked as a project manager for Morrison-Knudsen for the past decade. The Rio Blanco copper mine in Chile in 1973 and Inga-Shaba hydro dam in Zaire the year before were recent stopovers. "Pinochet and Mobutu are easy clients," he said to a colleague. "Only one person to answer to." His company constructed many of the engineering marvels of the twentieth century, including the Hoover Dam and St. Lawrence Seaway. Wells had one good thing to say about his current clients -- they didn't flirt with the Soviets, like Nasser did with Aswan. That made his job -- getting things built in out-of-the-way places – a lot easier. Luis Gajate had called him several weeks back about keeping an eye out for Beryl Thomas' brother.

In addition to managing big engineering projects in remote, unsettled places, Ziggy also looked out for government interests. He could always get someone to the front of the line at the U.S. embassy in Asuncion or red flag an issue to the right group at Langley. Ziggy had heard stories about bounties being given out for carrying escaped people back, but that sounded dramatic. "We don't see kidnapped kids up here," he told Luis. "It's too far from anywhere to matter. But I'll look into it. Name's Marcela Alvarez. Right? OK, she probably changed it, but we'll start there. There's a guy here in town who knows everything and everybody."

"Thanks," answered Luis. "How's the project going? Still a shit show?"

"We're beginning to pour footings next week, fingers crossed, Christ the Lord," Ziggy answered. "Everything's been smooth of late. Everyone's behaving, no surprises at least this week."

"Did you hear the news on Letelier?"

"Yeah, I saw it in the *Herald Tribune.* It was a DINA hit, using Cubans. Well I'll be, you could have knocked me over with a goddamn I-beam," he howled. "Took 'em a long time. The hitman was an American ... from Waterloo, Iowa. I've learned to stay away from those Chilean military guys. Crazy committed, but no guardrails. Blowing somebody up in the middle of Washington D.C.? What happened to a little poison in the mail like the old days?"

"Trial just started in January. I expect clarity on this assassination is not in anyone's best interest. We've seen it before."

"Indeed, we have. Ciao, brother. By the way, the guy in the Frontier is named Eduardo Maloof. Everyone seems to know him. Happy to make an intro if you'd like. He knows everything about this part of the world. He's a good sort."

Eduardo Maloof always made time for Marcela, ever since he spotted her in the post office that early summer day four months ago. She was a sunny new face that he took an instant liking to. Eduardo continued to bring her presents from across the river, although the last thing she needed was another locally-made Pioneer cassette deck or Renoir knock-off. Today, Eduardo was out checking a fence line where a caiman and a jaguar got into it over a marsh deer and tore through the barrier. Much of the land he had acquired was just dense tropical forest, useful only for wildlife. This land was going to be worth something one day and Eduardo Maloof was in no hurry. His partner across the river was more impatient, talking about resort hotels and gambling. "Slow down, we'll know it when we see it," he answered confidently, whenever questioned about his plans for the future. He was a generous neighbor, a town father and trustee of sorts. Getting rich quick was never his priority.

"Madame," he called through the screen windows. "The Parana River has been tamed again. Wildlife, for now, is held at bay," he proclaimed with a flourish. "Oh, who do we have here?" he stepped back, surprised to see a young man with a big moustache in uncomfortable slacks sitting on the porch. Or, rather, *his* porch. Eduardo stepped back, not knowing quite how to react.

Ricardo stood up immediately and offered his hand to Eduardo. He had been staying in a small room in the basement of the cottage for the last few weeks, while he looked for work. He only had $450 left and they had talked many times about making an introduction to Eduardo. Certainly, he needed help with his business empire? Marcela had told her brother about her arrival and meeting him in the post office and their friendship since. "I am her black sheep little brother, Ricardo," he smiled. "And you must be Eduardo Maloof?"

"Welcome to Foz. Your sister has been waiting for you to arrive here every day since I met her in the post office mailing a postcard to you. You are the entrepreneur I've heard lots about?" Eduardo proclaimed. "Certainly, the dresser in the family."

Ricardo stood, without words, smiling, "I'm not sure about that, but I like business challenges. I was involved in several restaurant ventures in Pocitos Beach. You've heard of it?"

Eduardo smiled, but shook his head. "I've heard about life in Pando before the military took over. And Marcela told me lots of stories about you and your sister Cristina. I'm so happy that the Alvarez family has made the Frontier their home. At least for now."

Ricardo grinned from ear to ear. "I've spent last few weeks looking around this town. It has potential. This area is primed to be the next major international tourist destination. I can feel it."

"That is music to my ears," Eduardo replied, somewhat surprised that this person was Marcela's brother. They were very different. "I've believed for years that his area can be a Las Vegas in the Jungle. Maybe even host the next Ali-Foreman fight? We must think big. What's the first thing that comes to your mind when I say Brazil?"

"Shapely women," Ricardo replied excitedly, moving his hands and winking his left eye. Marcela stood in the corner, shaking her head.

"What else?" Eduardo continued.

"Mmm, the Amazon River, the Andes, futbol, bossa nova music, and of course, Iguaçu Falls. The greatest falls in the world," Ricardo answered proudly.

"We need to study what they did to develop the infrastructure around Victoria Falls," Eduardo replied, encouraged by the talk. "It's one of the top tourism destination in Africa and it straddles two countries. There's an American engineer I know working on the dam who is worth talking to. We need to start researching how this was done. Five-star hotels and duty free shopping. This can be a special economic zone. That's what the Zambians and Rhodesians figured out."

Marcela quietly entered the room, listening to the men in her life excitedly talk about the future. They were happy and excited, each one one-upping the other on what could be. It was invigorating for her to hear the ascending scale of enthusiasm and a string of 'what-if's' as she brought drinks and sweets to her new family. Marcela was still sorting through the turns of her own her life and long ago swore off feeling sorry for herself. She was alive and safe and there was nothing she could do to bring back Paulo. Everyone has to go on and accept life's unpredictable turns, she had concluded, and both of these men celebrated vitality and lived for the future. She liked that Ricardo could have a life here and she'd never lose sight of him again.

Ricardo's arrival six weeks ago surprised everyone. He still dressed like a clown. His sister spotted him at the Falls, walking down the hill from Devil's Throat, where she painted a few days a week. At first, she didn't recognize him. He had put on weight and grown a moustache since she had seen him nearly two years ago. Ricardo was cheerful and full of dreams and schemes and, most importantly, he was her baby brother. He was young when Marcela left home, but now was an adult, still full of youth and humor. She liked that he still walked his own way. That he got her postcard, figured it out, and made it to Iguaçu made Marcela feel good and grateful. Her family intuitively understood a secret language and rallied in an impossible time.

Eduardo hired Ricardo that afternoon to be his special assistant. He laughed telling Ricardo that it was a bootleg copy of Milton Friedman's opus 'Capitalism and Freedom' that launched his business career more than two decades ago. He wasn't sure whether Ricardo was the book reading type – his instincts suggested otherwise, but the young man was eager, talked a good game, and was almost family. Eduardo had never trusted anyone to work with him, besides his cousin and the lazy receptionist. He'd always enjoyed being his own boss and keeping his own schedule. But he liked Ricardo's energy and he did need new blood to help him with his businesses. Everything had gotten more complicated now with the dam construction. Once it is completed and operating within a decade, what will this place be like?

The one trait Eduardo brought from the old country was an appreciation for land, no matter what condition it was in. There was something atavistic about land ownership to a Levantine. When Eduardo moved here, land was practically given away, so his extended Syrian family acquired vast hectares of cheap land around the national park. Eduardo really never thought about what he would do with the property. He'd just rather have it than not and his businesses were spinning off money and it had to go somewhere. Several people over the years approached Eduardo and he liked the idea of a theme park to attract visitors. Something will come along at the right time, he assured himself.

Despite his new title as Senior Manager, Special Projects, Ricardo's primary job was to drive Eduardo over the Friendship Bridge and sit quietly in the corner while two old men carried on about business and life. Ricardo learned that Eduardo stayed clear of the marijuana and cocaine trade for moral reasons, but dabbled in other sorts of cross-border contraband and money-laundering exchanges. Occasionally, he procured Swiss automatic pistols and Israeli IW1's for clients he deemed trustworthy and not connected to the Argentine government.

Ricardo and Eduardo chatted amiably on the ride over Friday morning to meet with several of his distribution partners. It was all about who could get Dunhill's, Chivas Regal and Paco Rabane to the streets of Rio and Sao Paulo first. Ricardo enjoyed the bombardment of consumer goods as they walked through the bazaar selling electronics, booze, clothes, perfumes, plumbing parts, M-16s, and acres of bright polyester fabric. The market was sticky, loud, and argumentative. There was a strange odor of cheap incense wafting through the tight alleys and Ricardo got the impression anything you imagined could be bought here. It was a souk in the middle of a jungle. Eduardo motioned ahead to a small shop a few hundred feet up the street from the crowded market. A hand-painted sign 'Shalhoub Travel Adventure Agency' hung in the window.

"Raimi, I want you to meet Ricardo, my new assistant. He's Marcela's brother and is helping me with special projects and our vision of bringing the world to the Frontier. *The New Frontier.* We've talked about it for years."

Raimi Shalhoub rose excitedly from his small desk in front of yellowing travel posters and thrust his hand toward Ricardo. He was plump, modestly dressed and wore thick black-rimmed glasses. Eduardo introduced him as his oldest friend and business partner without further explanation. Ricardo had heard from his sister that these Syrian Christians stuck together and were rich as Croesus.

Raimi smiled. "My job is to help get people *out* of here to other places, so we are in complementary businesses. Mr. Friedman would approve of the market efficiency. It's a pleasure to meet you." Raimi had a large round animated face, distorted by the bifocals, that grew wider as Eduardo handed him a zippered canvas duffle, neatly packed with several padded envelopes. He peeked at each packet, flipped through the pages, and nodded. "Your sister is very good. The best in the Frontier."

"Have you heard of bounty hunters operating in the Frontier?" Eduardo asked. "His sister escaped from one of those detention facilities and is worried they might be looking for her."

Raimi answered. "I doubt it. No one likes the Argentine police around here. I haven't heard of anyone, but I'll keep an ear out. I've got a full order for next week," Raimi relayed as he counted out $120 and sealed the bills in a white envelope. He handed Eduardo a packet with information and small black and white passport photos. "Seems like everyone wants out." He motioned to Ricardo in the corner. "Except you. I like you. Our new minister of tourism."

Ricardo beamed, although he was cautious not to get too far ahead of himself. It was his strength and weakness. He smiled and sat up, hoping for another opportunity to insert himself into the conversation. Eduardo was vague in describing his relationship with Raimi, but it was clear by the unspoken gestures to one another that their friendship went back decades. "Why can't we make this the duty free capital in the Amazon region?"

The two middle-aged men nodded as Ricardo rambled along, passionately. They had been buying land for over two decades. Free markets always brought about hope and opportunity. Now there was young blood with new ideas. Ricardo would take some getting used to, but the old men liked that all their land might finally be worth something.

"Gentlemen, you have an opportunity to create the standard for natural beauty and top flight entertainment in the world's most exotic location," Ricardo began 'imagineering' from his corner seat. "Look at Las Vegas! People come from all over the world to the middle of a desert just to gamble and watch Liberace. We have so much more: natural beauty, wild animals, the best of South America, all right here. All we need now are laws to get gambling reintroduced in the Frontier."

Raimi liked this young guy thinking about the future. Making gambling legal again had been discussed for years. It was a natural and would drive tourism. Neither he nor Eduardo could understood why the usually libertine Brazilian government would get so pious and moral about something so natural and obvious. "Aside from gambling, let's do some research on what the Southern Rhodesians and Zambians have done: hotels, boat cruises, rafting, safaris and bungee jumping. I saw on the news that some crazy Brit just jumped off a bridge in England last year with an elastic cord they call a *bungee*. It's perfectly safe. They use them to tow gliders. We should look into it."

"Let's make this an adventure destination," Ricardo began excitedly. "Come to the wilds of the deepest, darkest Amazon. See Iguazu Falls, exotic jaguars and caiman and win yourself a fortune."

Seventeen

March 1978

Foz do Iguaçu, Brasil

Sunday afternoon was feijoada time for the Alvarez family. The traditional slow-cooked stew of animal parts and black beans became a weekly occasion for all of them, as they began to piece together what they were going to do now. Ricardo instantly fell in with Eduardo and made plans for the future, but Cristina was stuck. This wasn't her home and now that everyone was safe, she wanted to practice architecture again. After six months without income, money was tight and she'd become moody and restless. Willie was already talking about heading back to the States to write his article on finding Marcela. It was a great story with a happy ending.

Marcela spent several afternoons talking to Willie and Cristina about her experience. She relayed her story precisely, remembering the long days and nights at Floresta, never holding back on the torture and day-to-day miseries. Her voice was strong, even when she spoke of Paulo and her unborn child. Willie jotted down every detail of the *picana* and *submarino* treatments, the degradations of blowjobs and awful names, of the constant feelings of fear and boredom. Her poise and articulation reminded him so much of Cristina. They were both fearless. It was a time for taking stock, recharging and figuring out what's next. Willie and Cristina had met with a U.S. consular officer in CDE two weeks ago that Ziggy set up. They could issue her a refugee visa to the United States, based on her family and situation. All she had to do was to fill the form out.

These decisions became more urgent the following week after Marcela saw the unmistakable stride of *el ejecutor* from a distance shuffling across the square. The gaucho belt was the giveaway, though he looked to have put on weight since she last saw him in December. Sánchez still wore the same stained khaki trousers, but had bought a new striped rayon shirt. The sighting made her sick to her stomach and it was only a matter of time before he'd find her. Marcela needed to stay out at the cottage and away from the Falls until they figured something out. The Argentine police were thorough, she had to admit. Marcela wondered if there were others hunting her as well. Maybe they got wind of the postcards? It was the best plan she could come up with, but now it seemed like a huge mistake. She had attracted the Argentine police to this faraway place, and now, her family was in danger.

"I'm telling you, I saw him, that miserable son of a bitch who tortured and raped me." Marcela was crying, recounting what she saw waddling across the square earlier today. "We've got a big problem. He's after me. God knows who else is."

The family listened carefully, except Ricardo who kept jumping up, swearing he would hunt this pig down and kill him with his bare hands. Cristina and Willie looked at each other alarmed and overwhelmed. Willie finally jumped in.

"I'm not so sure. This might work to our advantage. This guy has no power in Brazil. You said he didn't have a uniform on. He might be freelancing for a bounty. I read that in an Amnesty report."

"Then let's kill him right now," Ricardo argued. "He raped my sister."

"Willie's right on this," Cristina nodded. "He could try to kidnap Marcela and take her back. But he's got no jurisdiction and can't go to the Brazilian police. Remember he hasn't seen her yet. Let's think this out. Marcela stays out at the cottage until he goes away. He might look around for a few days, but he'll go on if he doesn't find her. Or else, we can take matters into our own hands. We agree he has to be stopped. I don't want to look over my shoulder for anyone."

Ricardo liked his sister's thinking. "Yeah, let's kidnap him. Show him what torture is. We can slice off his tiny penis and toss him in the Parana River."

The room went completely silent, as everyone realized they were now talking about murdering someone. Cristina looked at her siblings, trying to assess the next steps.

Marcela jumped in. "I want nothing to do with killing anyone. I've seen enough of that. But he has to be stopped. Can we turn him in to the Brazilian police?"

Willie had a suggestion. "He doesn't know me at all. He knows all of your names and he might have pictures of Cristina and Ricardo. Where did you see him in town?"

"He was walking across the square by himself," Marcela replied. "He looked to be alone. Almost looks like he's on vacation."

"OK then. I'll go into town and do some of my own detective work," Willie volunteered. "We know the military arrests young people, drugs them, takes them up in helicopters and tosses them into the Rio Plata. Time for a little turnabout. Where can we get sodium pentothal?"

Marcela stood and put the palms of her hands out. "We can't do this. It's vengeance. We have to be better than they are. Or he is."

"That's all well and good," Ricardo answered. "But we don't know who sent him, or if there are others. I vote that we take him out before anything else happens. Or figures out she's here and calls in the local police."

Cristina watched them argue, agitatedly listening to the building emotion and bloodthirst. She agreed with her sister, but what could they do about Marcela's torturer? He had to be stopped. "Are you positively sure that this person you saw in the square was the man who tortured and raped you?"

"Yes, I am certain. That is an indelible image, I'm sorry to say. Do what you have to do. I want nothing to do with it."

Willie had no trouble finding the Argentine. Marcela's description of Rafael Sánchez was dead on. He was staying at the Hotel Teresopolis on Rua Barroso. He had checked in three days ago and taken a tour of the Falls yesterday. Last night, he ate at the Restaurant Italia next to the Rodoviaria. He had a late night drink at the Bier Haus along Kubitschek after dinner. That was the report from Eduardo, who insisted that this man be followed. "I don't like Argentine police on our soil to begin with. Let me know if you need additional assistance."

The urgency for revenge was real and now Willie and Ricardo travelled silently over the gravel road south towards town. Sánchez had paid for a single room for the week, according to Eduardo's sources. After that, it wasn't clear. The good news is that he was traveling alone. "Like we discussed, I'll make contact with him," Willie said. "He's gone to that German bar both nights, so we'll start there and hope we find him. I'll strike up a conversation with him and slip the pentothal into his drink. He'll be drowsy and disoriented in twenty minutes. Just another drunk tourist. He'll stagger back to his hotel and you can be waiting outside with the car."

Ricardo nodded. "But the bartender might ID you? He might say that the policeman was last seen in the company of an American tourist?"

"That is the risk, if there is an investigation. I suspect no one will care. The bigger question is what will we do with him," shrugged Willie.

"That's not a problem," Ricardo answered. "Mr. Maloof has agreed to help us with the disposal process. That fucker will pay for raping my sister and for trying to hunt me and Cristina down. Marcela doesn't need to know the details."

As they approached the outskirts of town, Willie began to have second thoughts about what they were preparing to do. The adrenalin had plateaued. He hadn't really thought about this as a crime, but more of a duty. This man deserved to die for his sins. It was as simple as that. Willie knew he needed to toughen up and rise to the occasion.

"Give me an hour," Willie said, getting out of the car two blocks from the center of town. "I'll look for you at the Rodoviaia around 9:30. OK?"

The Bier Haus was mostly empty. It was a Tuesday night. Willie tried to relax and keep his cool as he sat down at the bar, two stools away from a plump, sweaty man nursing a liter of Brahma. "Good evening," Willie said politely. "Is anyone sitting here?"

The man shook his head and smiled, gesturing toward the bar stool. "No, go ahead. Free country."

"Thank you," Willie smiled gritting his teeth at the tone of the remark, confirming his instant dislike for the man.

"American? English?"

"American. I'm here on vacation. The falls are more beautiful than the postcards."

The man nodded and sipped his beer. "I like America. Strong country. John Wayne."

Willie had not heard that name in ages. Was he still doing movies? The last one was about the Green Berets, he thought he remembered. Willie shot him the thumbs up sign and continued sipping his beer. "The falls on the Brazilian side are more spectacular, but the Argentine side is more interesting. Lots of little falls."

"Yes, the Argentine side is much better. I say that because I'm Argentine," he laughed.

"Where are you from?" Willie asked.

"Buenos Aires," he answered proudly. "I'm on vacation too. But I must carve out some time while I'm here for work. I'm a policeman. My name's Rafael."

"Hi, I'm William. What brings you here?"

"Tracking down Argentine socialist agitators. I'm here to locate a missing person, an escaped prisoner."

"I noticed some women in the main square in BA protesting about missing people. What's that about?'

"Just socialists trying to get something for nothing. If they worked as hard as they protested, they might be wealthy like other Argentines."

"Yes, it is a wonderful country. Far nicer and more civilized than America."

"I read that people get shot in the streets in New York City," Sánchez replied.

"Sometimes, America can be a dangerous place. That's why people carry guns."

Rafael didn't quite know how to answer the comment. Of course, Americans carry guns. He had seen enough movies to know that much. "Like *The French Connection*? Pop, pop, pop," he smiled, putting his trigger finger on a new pint of Brahma. The conversation had gotten Sánchez excited and he excused himself to use the toilet, back towards the kitchen.

Everything had gone as Willie hoped. He watched Sánchez waddle toward the bathroom, as the barman turned toward the wall to identify a bottle of Fernet for another customer. Carefully, he pulled a small packet out of his jacket and dissolved its contents into the pint of Brahma. A small fizz that seemed to last for hours finally dissipated, just as Sánchez returned from the toilet, shirt tucked in, his belt neatly holding in his girth.

Sánchez took another sip of his beer. He looked unsettled. "This Brazilian beer tastes like cat piss. You should try a Quilmes if you get back to BA. Far better than this", he scoffed, then gulped the remainder of the beer down. The bartender stared over at his customer as he shouted for another round. "What else do you have on tap? How about a Salta Lager? Or a Schneider? Anything from Argentina?"

The barman shrugged. It seemed like hours, but Sánchez finished two pints of Salta quickly. He began to slur his words and his criticism of everything not Argentine got louder. The other patrons at the bar rolled their eyes at the pudgy visitor. The other customers began to notice a very drunk and sweaty man, moving his upper body erratically. "Just one more, barkeep," he yelled to the man four feet away.

"Sorry, sir. I'm not going to be able to serve you anymore."

"Fuck you," Sánchez answered, as he tried to stand up.

"It's time for you to go, sir. You've had enough to drink tonight."

Willie quickly jumped in. "Friend, can I help get you back to your hotel? You don't look well."

"They must spike the beer here," he answered, voice slurring, body wobbly.

Willie put his arm around Sánchez's back and tried to get him to stand up. "Where's your hotel?"

The barman, glad to be rid of this cheap drunk who hadn't tipped him the last two nights, smiled and put his hands together in mock-prayer. "Please take him away from here. Put him on a bench. Maybe the street sweeper will take him away."

"Happy to."

Willie led him from the bar and pushed him into the Fiat on the quiet side street. "I may have overdone the portions," Willie apologized. "I got a C minus in Chemistry." He looked back at the hunk of blubber spread out across the back seat. "He's a disgusting excuse for a human being." he continued. "What do we do with him?"

"We need to disappear him," Ricardo answered. "Just like we discussed." He spoke softly as an intensity came over his face, shifting into third gear. "No time for second thoughts."

They drove north in silence toward the dam along the paved road leading out of town. It was always easier to talk about something, rather than actually doing it. That had been Willie's weakness all along. Thinking, talking, not doing. They must follow through now. The cop was out like a light across the back seat of the Fiat. Eduardo indicated that there was a gravel service road for the large trucks delivering rebar and concrete to the site up on the edge of the park fifteen minutes away. It was dark and the road surface was uneven. Far ahead on the horizon, Willie could see enormous cranes and tractors along the shoreline through the moonlight. "Anything that goes in here," Ricardo motioned off to his left, "eventually ends up in the Rio Plata. In a few weeks-time, what's left of this son-of-a-bitch will be in the Atlantic Ocean where he can join his victims. Miserable bastard."

Ricardo pulled up to the edge of the escarpment. An eerie moonglow came over the treetops and the mighty Parana River from 200 feet above looked tiny and sinewy, the currents reflecting little sparkles of light. "Too late for reconsideration," he shrugged awkwardly. "Let's get this over with."

Ricardo and Willie dragged Rafael Sánchez to the edge of the cliff. Ricardo stuck his shoe under the damp body and levered the lump over the edge. A few seconds later, they heard a distant thump as the body hit rocks and finally, a splash. They looked grimly at each other and got back in the car for the drive down the hill towards his sister's. It was done. They drove in silence to the cottage, the expected sense of relief and vengeance had yet to materialize and the weight of what they did, now hung heavy in the thick, humid air. It was done, they had told themselves. It was either him or them – he planned to bring Marcela back, dead or alive. Maybe even her brother and sister as well? He wouldn't be missed by anyone. But still, they had just murdered a human being and, justified or not, that made Willie Thomas sick to his stomach.

Later that night, Willie sat on the porch, listening to the thundering waters, thinking about what he had done. Everyone else was in bed except Cristina, who was sitting on the porch blowing smoke rings into the air. It wasn't over for her. She now was 'wanted' by the Argentine government. Would they send another soldier out to silence them? Marcela had begun to share her gruesome stories over the past few weeks. Cristina could not imagine being tortured for a year-and-a-half for doing nothing wrong. It was hard to get her head around the notion that her sister had been 'lucky. She used to love her country.

She squeezed Willie's hand firmly, almost desperately. "Where am I going to go? I can't stay here. I love my family, but I need to go back to work. I'm broke. I'm bored."

"You could come to the States," Willie suggested again. This was old territory. "You surely have grounds to request asylum. You have family there. We've talked about this before. It's your only choice. Particularly after what we just did. We need to get to the U.S. as soon as we can. There's a chance they could find the body. A very slim chance."

"I don't want to go to America. I've told you that. I want to go back to my job in BA. I want things to be normal." Cristina had been crying for the past hour, petrified about her future. She slid over and tucked her head on Willie's shoulder. "I just want things to go back to normal. Is that too much to ask?"

Willie put his arm around her and rubbed her shoulder and hair. "No, it's not. Come to the States. It's the only safe place for you right now." The light breeze coming through the screen smelled of jasmine and gardenias. "Just until this period is over. Then you can go back and rebuild Buenos Aires."

"Funny how things turn out," she chuckled in frustration, throwing her hands up. "Now it's me who doesn't know what to do, or where to go." She turned to Willie, resigned. "I'll go, you're right. It's the only option."

"Great, you'll see it's for the best," Willie smiled. "The American guy that Luis mentioned can get you an asylum hearing at the Embassy in Asunción anytime."

"I know, thank you. I've been a pain, but I know I need to get on with my life. The only reason I could come up with for staying here is to design Ricardo's theme park. I love him, but we'd kill each other." Cristina had calmed down as Willie rubbed the back of her neck.

"Trust me. Everything's going to work out."

Willie needed assurances too. What would he tell people he'd been doing the past two years? His spiral bound notebook was filled with information on bus routes, torture chambers, the secret Condor network, plus a cursory history of Uruguay and Argentina, including the differences between the Montoneros and the Tupamaros, and the mostly disastrous role the Catholic Church played in the dirty war. He interviewed Marcela who courageously recounted the details of her own torture. Willie had collected newspaper articles on the various assassinations and catalogued numerous Amnesty reports. He learned which hotels and hostels have the hottest water. How all of it would come together was a whole other matter, but the research phase was done. He was hopeful Cristina would be there to look over his shoulder to make sure the final story was told well.

"Leave home" was the advice the author Paul Theroux gave in an *Esquire* article when asked about becoming a writer. Willie had done that. Throughout most of the trip, he devoted an hour a day to his journal. At first, it was impossible to fill more than a half page. It was all facts and figures; the sites, their prices and addresses, where they ate and stayed. Then increasingly his entries became conversations and the different opinions he was picking up along the way. Cristina was always going to make this a story worth reading. He continued to follow the news of Orlando Letelier's murder trial, where he could. It turned out to be a DINA hit, just as Alma said that rainy morning. Pinochet gave up the American and the Republic of Chile suffered no punishment for this or any of the Operation Condor murders. Townley cut a deal and got his wrists slapped -- a few years in a federal prison in Colorado and a new identity. The Cubans were hung out to dry and convicted for the murders, although they couldn't find one of the hit men. The verdict was unsatisfying, but predictable. Pinochet had survived and avoided stepping on the banana peel.

It had been three weeks since Rafael Sánchez was drugged and tossed into the Parana River. No one missed him. It was an impetuous act and a crime, although Willie had reasoned it out enough for him to sleep at night. *El ejecutor* presented himself as a threat and they acted in self-defense; it was either him or them. Willie did wonder how this memory would carry into the future? He left the

United States seven months ago hoping to avoid decisions about his future. Was he prepared to live with this secret forever? As much as he tried, the thumping sound of Rafael Sánchez hitting the edge of the steep cliff on his descent occasionally replayed in his mind. It had taken both of them to pull Sánchez out of the car and drag him to the edge. One night last week, Willie dreamt that Sánchez somehow survived the fall and was coming for him. All he could do was to hope the memory kept fading.

Cristina and Willie drove to Asunción to pick up her approved asylum papers from the Embassy. Her sister joked that she could produce an American passport in a few hours, saving her the daylong drive, but Cristina resisted. "I'm keeping my Argentine passport and citizenship for another day. Hopefully not far in the future, I'll use it again." Cristina planned out her new American future like any problem that needed solving. She spent several hours on the telephone talking to her partners in BA about her predicament. She couldn't come back, at least for a while. Could they introduce her to Robert Venturi, an American architect she'd always admired? His firm was located in Philadelphia and they had just won a new client, the City of Houston who planned to build a new children's art museum. A week later, she got a response. "They would love to talk to you," her partner said over a telephone call. "We'll be glad to send your portfolio onto them. You are destined to design that museum. It won't be built anytime soon in this hellhole. Stay away, for now."

Ricardo settled into a job with Eduardo as a 'general associate' in charge of growth opportunities. There was money to be made here, real money, he could tell that just by breathing the air. He had big ideas for making Foz do Iguaçu a travel destination for Brazilian-themed music and entertainment, including an Amazon waterpark, an annual 'Jungle Sambafest', and a Jaguar Safari. Eduardo wasn't always sure about what Ricardo was going on about, the boy could talk a blue streak. But he liked him and Marcela deserved to have some of her family around. He needed someone young who he could trust. That was the only accepted currency in the Triple Frontier.

Eighteen

Chantilly, VA.

Late April 1978

Haze hung over the green Virginia countryside. It was spring and the summer humidity was coming. Willie looked out of the window of the Varig flight, cutting through the morning clouds. The pilot was making final announcements about their arrival. Willie was excited to be coming home after eight months. He had his adventure, and then some. He looked over at Cristina, who had been drinking coffee and doodling throughout the night. She was still drawing elevations for her children's museum, seemingly unaware that they were landing in the United States. Willie pointed out the porthole at the sloping, graceful concrete structure, shaped like the wing of an airplane.

Cristina sat up excitedly and leaned across Willie as the plane gently touched down. She could see the shining Dulles International Airport terminal in the morning light, practically beckoning her to visit. "It's beautiful. What a structure! Eero Saarinen was a genius," she said contentedly. "What a wonderful morning." The plane slowly taxied in toward the terminal as the crew made announcements about custom's procedures in Portuguese and English. Cristina hadn't slept in over twenty-four hours, but she was excited and wide awake. "I like his TWA terminal at Kennedy better, but this is spectacular."

Willie put his arm around her shoulder. "Welcome to the United States," he whispered into her ear. "Don't worry, like I said, it will work out fine. Somebody's going to want to build your museum here."

Two enthusiastic women stood behind the barrier at the arrivals building holding a big sign saying WELCOME HOME WILLIE AND CRISTINA. They were hopping up and down, particularly the small, dark-haired woman in a bright fuchsia dress. The taller blond-haired woman in blue jeans and clogs waved her hands as the procession of bleary-eyed travelers made their way through the baggage claim area.

Cristina looked up and screamed, "Auntie, auntie," as she ran to give Alma a hug. The other woman ran to give Willie a hug. "Welcome home, baby bro," she shouted, grabbing him around the shoulders. Willie returned the embrace that went on for close to a minute. He turned and hugged Alma, as tears came into his eyes. She whispered in his ear, "You saved my family. You are a hero." His sister looked over at him and nodded with an approving smile.

Willie blushed. He never thought of himself as a hero. But at least he tried something. He just turned twenty-five and remembered his sister saying that the line to the rat race was much shorter now. He needed to tell her everything, or almost everything. What started as an escape to South America to write a travel guidebook took a strange turn. It had become a tale worth telling.

James Bell

Epilogue

The dictatorships and intelligence services of the member countries behind Operation Condor were responsible for tens of thousands of killed and missing people in the period between 1975 and 1985. Brazilian journalist Nilson Mariano estimates the number of killed and missing people as upwards of 30,000 in Argentina, 10,000 in Chile, 500 in Bolivia, 1,000 in Brazil, 400 in Paraguay, and 250 in Uruguay. The Dirty War lasted for nearly a decade, ending in 1983 after the Falklands War defeat sent the shamed Argentine dictatorship to jail. Chile followed suit with a 1988 plebiscite that tossed Augusto Pinochet out of power.

As a relative comparison, 48,000 U.S. soldiers were killed in Viet Nam between 1964-1975. The scale of what happened in the Southern Cone has never been completely understood and explained.

Michael Townley was sentenced to ten years, with credit for time served, in accordance with his plea bargain in exchange for testimony in the Orlando Letelier murder trial. He received a new identity and was confined to an undisclosed medium security prison, until his parole in October 1981. As of 2015, he remained alive in the witness protection program.

Guillermo and Ignacio Novo were convicted in the murder of Orlando Letelier and Ronni Moffit in 1978, but were acquitted in a new trial because of inconsistencies in testimony from jailhouse informants a year later. In 2000, Guillermo Novo and three Cuban exile colleagues were arrested for attempting to assassinate Fidel Castro at the University of Panama.

Virgilio Paz was convicted *in absentia* for the murder of Orlando Letelier and he lived under the assumed name 'Francisco Luis (Frank) Baez' outside West Palm Beach. He was active in the community and owned a landscaping business. On April 24, 1991, he was captured without incident as he drove to work a few days after his story was told on an episode of *America's Most Wanted*. He pleaded guilty in the conspiracy to assassinate Letelier, and was sentenced to 12 years in prison.

General Manuel Contreras, former head of Chile's DINA was convicted in November, 1993 for murdering Orlando Letelier and sentenced to seven years in prison. Contreras subsequently was convicted of several other murders and died behind bars in 2015.

General Augusto Pinochet stepped down from the presidency of Chile in 1990 after being voted out of office in a 1988 plebiscite. He was arrested in London in 1998 for numerous human rights violations and returned to Chile. He died in 2006 at the age of 91, with over 300 criminal charges still pending against him. He was never charged in Letelier's murder.

General Rafael Videla was convicted of numerous crimes in 1985 including homicide, kidnapping and torture and was sentenced to life imprisonment. He died in 2013 from natural causes in the Marcos Paz prison outside Buenos Aires.

Eugene Propper is a retired private practice attorney, living in South Carolina with his wife and two dogs.

Bob Scherrer, described by colleagues as 'an intelligence center all by himself,' died in 1995 at age 60 in Palm Coast, Florida. From 1970-1978, he was assistant legal attaché for the FBI posted in Buenos Aires. He returned to Washington until retiring in 1987.

Carter Cornick retired from the FBI in 1988 after a twenty-year career as a counter terrorism specialist and lives in Virginia.

Marcela Rezende continues to paint in the Triple Frontier. She also works for Eduardo Maloof, creating counterfeit passports and promotional and marketing materials for Samba Land, a theme park, run by her brother Ricardo. She never remarried or returned to Buenos Aires.

Cristina Alvarez moved to Philadelphia to restart her career as an architect in 1978. Her first project for Venturi, Scott Brown, and Partners was The Children's Museum of Houston. In 1985, she returned to Buenos Aires and set up her own practice. She too never married.

Willie Thomas sold his 20,000 word story, 'Living After Disappearing' to *Esquire* Magazine in 1979. He continued to contribute to *Esquire, The New Yorker* Magazine, and other periodicals throughout an ongoing career in journalism and travel writing.

Afterword

Like my protagonist, I knew nothing about South America in 1976. It was a huge, lopsided ice cream cone, an overnight plane ride south. I remember hearing about the Incas, the Andes, Pizarro, and Jose San Martin in school, and then Pele came along. A few years later, *Evita* opened on Broadway and the movie *Missing*, starring Sissy Spacek and Jack Lemmon about disappearances in Chile in 1973, was released. I'd heard of Pinochet and Stroessner, only because they appeared out of central casting as right wing military dictators from faraway places -- mid-century relics still sputtering along as the Cold War petered out in the late 1980s. They certainly awarded themselves a lot of medals.

After that, it was a blur. In the late seventies, we began to see short, gritty black and white newscasts of women carrying signs with pictures of their children in the main square in Buenos Aires. I vaguely remember the war in the Falkland Islands a few years later, when the world got to see what a venal pack of idiots the Argentine military dictatorship turned out to be. Argentina returned to elected democracy in 1983. Pinochet and Stroessner hung on until the late 1980s, and both died in shame over the last decade.

The impetus for this story sprang from my curiosity about South America, our continental neighbor composed of twelve countries we've never gone to war with, at least directly. My experiences began in the early 1990s. I've been fortunate to get to know wonderful people and places in Peru, Chile, Argentina, and Brazil over a twenty-year period of regularly going there for work. I did manage to spend a bizarre day in Ciudade de Este, Paraguay, the home of Iguaçu Falls and can begin to understand Graham Greene's reference to the country as 'an island, surrounded by land.'

I began writing this book by typing words and names into the Google machine. Lo and behold, what came back was a historical fiction writer's dream: a Wikipedia heading on something called OPERATION CONDOR. Then, another entry called DIRTY WAR. One article led to another to another that led to several books, then more books, almost twenty in all. Like my protagonist, in six months I had basic knowledge about a faraway land in our time zone and a brutal assassination 100 miles from where I typed this book. Orlando Letelier's murder remained the deadliest foreign terrorist attack on U.S. soil until the first World Trade center bombing in 1993.

Researching this book was disturbing. The prevalence and variety of torture used on young female citizens is repeatedly described in gaudy detail. They were raped, forced to carry children, and then had their babies snatched and given to military officers. For nearly a decade, this was an unknown and untold life for many in Argentina.

My enjoyment in writing books derives from researching a specific time period and place and then trying to figure out a story to tell. It was harder this time. The still-underreported human rights abuses that took up to 45,000 lives and ruined generations of citizens were upsetting to read and still feel unresolved. The Amnesty International and survivor accounts (acknowledged to be less than 10% of those 'disappeared') left me wondering if I could write a story about this era that captured the scale and brutality of what happened. The lively slang of *picanas* (electric cattle prods), *parrillas* (grills), and *submarinos* (water boarding) made these torture techniques seem almost normal in their casual familiarity and use.

The decade-long events that lasted from the early-seventies until Falklands War in 1982 are still being unpacked and accounted for. It was as though a part of the civilized world lost its humanity and the rest of the world just couldn't see or didn't bother noticing.

This was a time of Henry Kissinger's *real politik* and the end of the Viet Nam war. The mid-to-late seventies were hard-bitten times and even harder to romanticize: oil shocks, ugly clothes, Jim Jones and The People's Temple in Guyana, poorly-made domestic cars, U.S. cities going broke, Idi Amin, 'Stagflation', Son of Sam, the rise of the Khmer Rouge and Ayatollah Khomeini, and our 'national malaise.' South America's answer to the Asian civil wars was to double down on their militaries, rather than face longstanding structural economic imbalances. Their prototypes were the Catholic Church and Nazi Germany.

There was a glimmer of hope and redemption reading articles about Michelle Bachelet, the President of Chile from 2006-2010 and 2014-2018. She currently serves as the U.N. High Commissioner for Human Rights. She, her mother and sisters were held for a lengthy time at Villa Grimaldi, a notorious prison on the outskirts of Santiago, where her father was tortured and killed. She spoke of her torture, 'it was nothing in comparison to what the others suffered.'

The starting point for this novel began with researching the times and the places. Thankfully there are a wide variety of books and periodicals, that include Taylor Branch and Gene Propper's 'Labyrinth', Charles River Editors' 'Operation Condor', Bruce Chatwin's' 'On Patagonia', David Cox's 'Dirty Secrets, Dirty War' and Geoff Crowder's 'South America on a Shoestring.' In addition, I read a collection of different viewpoints on the time, place, and plot situation including 'Good Hunting' by Jack Devine, James Dickey's 'Deliverance', 'The Condor Years' by John Dinges, 'Assassination on Embassy Row' by Saul Landau and John Dinges, John Gimlette's "At the Tomb of the Inflatable Pig: Travels through Paraguay", Andrew Graham-Yool's 'A State of Fear: Memories of Argentina's Nightmare', Jennifer Harbury's 'Truth, Torture and the American Way', Daniel Lodel's 'Hades Argentina', 'Ghosts of Sheridan Circle' by Alan McPherson, Patrice McSherry's 'Predatory States: Operation Condor and Covert War in Latin America', Stephen Rabe's 'The Killing Zone', John Simpson and Jana Bennett's 'The Disappeared and the Mothers of the Plaza', Jacobo Timerman's 'Chile: Death in the South' and 'Prisoner

Without a Name, Cell Without a Number' and Patricia Verdugo's 'Chile, Pinochet and the Caravan of Death.'

As I have said with past efforts, it takes a small village to write these books. It always begins and ends with Heidi, my wife of thirty-six years, muse and toughest critic. This was no exception and she guided -- and chided -- me throughout this process again. David DeCamp and Ned Carter, lifelong friends, helped me with all things Washington D.C. and provided terrific counsel along the way. David in particular gave feedback throughout the writing process and should consider book editing as a second career. Marcela Villanueva, a friend and former colleague gave me some great insights on growing up around that period in Buenos Aires – and helped with Spanish. Old friend and former New York Lippincott colleague Julia McGreevy did the same, helping with the nuances of Brazilian Portuguese (as she ably did in Brazil fifteen years ago for our clients, Vale and Petrobras.) Sally Neill always provides fresh, clear and thoughtful advice on the story and characters. Randy Blake gave a personal perspective on the complexities and tragedies of war zone journalism. Once again, David Peterson helped me refine the plotline and a lot of this final story is thanks to him. Lastly Ross Howell, an old friend, editor, and author of the novel 'Forsaken,' which was a finalist for the 2017 Southern Book Prize in Historical Fiction, suggested several ideas that improved the overall story, as he has done on my prior six efforts. And last, certainly not least, Barb Wallace once again brought her vision to the cover design, for the seventh time. To all of you in different capacities who helped, thank you!

I hope that I have represented the spirit and events of this era fairly and accurately. The citizens of Argentina, Uruguay and Chile suffered in many ways and today the facts of what went on during this strange, lawless time continue to emerge.

Thank you very much for your time.

James Bell

Charlottesville, Virginia

Spring 2022

James Bell

About the Author

James Bell is an author who lives in Charlottesville, Virginia with his wife of 36 years. Prior to becoming a full time writer, James was a senior executive in the advertising and brand management consulting fields in New York City for over three decades.

His prior six novels include 'The Screen Door: A Story of Love, Letters & Travel' (2011), 'The Twenty Year Chafe' (2013), 'Christchurch' (2014), 'Crisis in the Congo' (2015), 'American Dreamer' (2019), and Spook (2020). They received effusive blanket praise from a small, yet insightful group of friends and strangers. 'Condor' is James' fourth work of historical fiction.

James Bell

James Bell

Made in the USA
Columbia, SC
03 April 2022

58345586R00166